PINK SMOG

Also by
FRANCESCA LIA BLOCK:

WEETZIE BAT

MISSING ANGEL JUAN

GIRL GODDESS #9: NINE STORIES

THE HANGED MAN

DANGEROUS ANGELS: THE WEETZIE BAT BOOKS

I WAS A TEENAGE FAIRY

VIOLET & CLAIRE

GUARDING THE MOON

WASTELAND

GOAT GIRLS: TWO WEETZIE BAT BOOKS

BEAUTIFUL BOYS: TWO WEETZIE BAT BOOKS

NECKLACE OF KISSES

BLOOD ROSES

HOW TO (UN)CAGE A GIRL

THE WATERS & THE WILD

PRETTY DEAD

THE FRENZY

HOUSE OF DOLLS

ROSES AND BONES: MYTHS, TALES, AND SECRETS

PINK SMOG
Becoming Weetzie Bat

FRANCESCA LIA BLOCK

An Imprint of HarperCollinsPublishers

HarperTeen is an imprint of HarperCollins Publishers.

∾❧∾

Pink Smog

Copyright © 2012 by Francesca Lia Block

Library of Congress Cataloging-in-Publication Data
Block, Francesca Lia.
    Pink smog : becoming Weetzie / Francesca Lia Block. — 1st ed.
        p.   cm.
    Prequel to: Weetzie Bat.
    Summary: When Weetzie Bat is a thirteen-year-old junior high
school outcast mourning the life her family lost when their cottage
in the Los Angeles hills burned down, her father leaves her alcoholic
mother without telling either of them where he is going and Weetzie
learns how to stand up for herself and to find beauty in even the most
difficult situations.
    ISBN 978-0-06-156598-4
    [1. Self-reliance—Fiction. 2. Fathers and daughters—Fic-
tion. 3. Divorce—Fiction. 4. Individuality—Fiction. 5. Junior
high schools—Fiction. 6. Schools—Fiction. 7. Los Angeles
(Calif.)—Fiction.]   I. Title.
PZ7.B61945Pi   2012   2011010028
[Fic]—dc22

Typography by Torborg Davern
11 12 13 14 15   CG/RRDH   10 9 8 7 6 5 4 3 2 1
❖
First Edition

FOR MY FAMILY,

GILDA AND IRVING BLOCK (TOGETHER IN MEMORY),

GREGG MARX, JASMINE, AND SAM

PINK SMOG

SLAM

The day after my dad, Charlie, the love of my life, left, and an angel saved my mom from drowning, I woke up with a slamming headache and a wicked sunburn.

When I checked on my mom she was asleep, breathing normally in the bed with the blue satin quilted headboard, so I got myself a bowl of Lucky Charms. The pink hearts, yellow moons, orange stars, and green clovers ached my molars as the milk turned rainbow colors. I made my lunch, brushed my teeth, and put on my roller skates. The pavement rumbled, rough under my feet and up through to my heart, as I skated to school past the palm trees that my dad said looked like stupid birds, under a smog-filled Los Angeles sky.

Miss Spinner sat on her stool with her long legs wrapped around each other three times as if they were made of rubber. She hissed at us to be quiet as she handed back our papers about summer vacation. Mine was called "Pink Smog." I had written about the pink sunset that we watched from the balcony where my parents drank their evening cocktails. They drank too many and stumbled around the condo fighting like a cat and a dog. Miss Spinner had written on my paper in red ink that fighting like a cat and a dog was a cliché and that the whole thing was "a bit much" but she made me read it out loud anyway.

"Louise," she said, "please stand up and read for us. Class, Louise's paper is an example of overwriting. Most of you under-write. I do not want you to overwrite either."

"Weetzie," I whispered. "My name's Weetzie."

My mom had named me for the silent movie star Louise Brooks, but it always felt too formal and mature for me. My dad called me Weetzie for no particular reason except that it was a diminutive and just sounded right, better for me than Lu or Lou-Lou or Weezie or Weez. Maybe because I am little and scrawny and it sounded a bit like my favorite cartoon character, Tweetie Bird. Teenie Weenie Tweeting Louise: Weetzie. Weird, but it fit.

There were a lot of things about me that might seem weird to people. I wondered why I hadn't written about going to Disneyland or something normal for Miss Spinner, even though my family hadn't even been to Magic Mountain or any other amusement park for that matter. We had just spent the whole summer at the pool, with my parents drinking and fighting and now the fighting had turned into a war and my dad was A.W.O.L. I wished I had just made something up about Disneyland and under-written it. As I read, the blood rushed to my face and it made my sunburn sting and my head pound even more.

"'In L.A. the sunsets are pink,'" I read. "'When the sun goes down and the sky flares it is really beautiful, like magic. However, the lush-plush-peony-rose of the L.A. sky is a by-product of something that may be killing us all, little by little. Smog! And smog is like sadness. It slips stealthily inside of you, with every breath, poisoning you before you realize it, kind of like the witch's apple in "Snow White," except even more discreet.'"

Staci Nettles, the prettiest girl in seventh grade, rolled her eyes and flipped her hair back over her shoulders. Then, when Miss Spinner turned away, Staci blew the biggest bubble-gum bubble I had ever seen, snapped it back in, and showed her perfect little white fangs with a smile that looked as if she had never been sad in her whole life.

Mr. Adolf was known for always starting his seventh graders off with a unit about World War II and whenever he talked about Hitler he got really excited and practically started jumping up and down. Spittle flew out of his mouth and he smoothed down the lock of greased hair that kept falling into his face as he told us about how the Jews were taken for "showers" when actually they were getting gassed to death. I sat there in the back of the class where the kids who wanted to disappear tried to hide, doodling pictures of my dad's convertible yellow Thunderbird with my pink pen, until Mr. Adolf told me to pay attention. I knew my problems were nothing compared to the Jews in Hitler's Germany but that thought did not cheer me up at all—the idea of Hitler's Germany was enough to depress even the happiest person. I thought of raising my hand and telling Mr. Adolf that my dad's grandmother had probably died in a concentration camp but I decided not to—he already didn't seem to like me very much.

At PE I dragged myself around the track for-what-felt-like-ever while Coach Pitt yelled at me. My legs are so spindly and knock-kneed, what did she expect? The only thing worse than running around and around in the smog was taking showers in public. Staci Nettles stood next to me with her hands in the air, wrapping a towel around her head, her big boobs in my face, her mouth in a Bonne Bell cherry-flavored lip-gloss smirk. I didn't waste time drying off—it meant being naked longer—so I struggled to pull my dress over my still-damp, pancake-flat chest as fast as I could. It is hard to not have breasts when everyone else seems to be growing them, especially when your mom looks like a Jayne Mansfield pinup like mine.

At lunch I sat alone as I had for the last week, since seventh grade started, watching the clock and eating the lunch I'd made—an apple and a pack of orange cheese spread and crackers. At least being alone was better than trying to be friends with mean girls. The ones who seemed nice were mostly sitting alone like I was and I felt too shy to go over to any of them, although I did smile at Lily Chin who was gnawing greedily on an apple and had a faint layer of dark down all over her body, like a baby animal. She smiled back shyly as if she was trying not to show her teeth.

I hadn't always been alone. Up until the end of sixth grade I'd gone to a cute little school in the canyon, called Wonderland. My best friends were twins named Skye and Karma Grier. They had moved away to Oregon because their mom, a singer/songwriter, and their dad, an artist, didn't want them to have to face the atrocities of public junior high school. Karma and Skye were tiny and brown-skinned with light hazel eyes and huge blonde Afros. We used to spend hours and hours playing in their organic vegetable garden, running through the sprinklers, baking granola cookies with their mother, Joy, gathering wildflowers to fill the house, making clothes out of scraps of old dresses, rags, leaves, tinfoil, and tissue paper and helping Marvin tile the patio with broken pottery, coins, and bottle caps. I loved being with Skye and Karma—it was almost like having siblings. I never felt alone.

But it had all changed overnight. Junior high was

like the bad kind of Wonderland in Alice where people are mean and crazy, everything is backward, and you're growing (hips) and shrinking (self-esteem) all the time.

In Mr. Gibbous's math class my skin hurt, my head hurt. The sunburn raged where the back of my thighs touched the plastic seat. I couldn't stay still. Mr. Gibbous stomped around, stammering loudly at us to stop fidgeting and be quiet while he scratched his head so that chunks of dandruff snowed onto his shoulders. He would have been a handsome man but he wore really weird, thick glasses and polyester pants that were short enough for a flood, and there were sweat stains under his arms, and the dandruff, of course. A walking target for junior high school kids. I wished I could find a way to tell him. He had been pretty nice to me so far, although he got exasperated and out of breath when I missed a problem, which had already happened kind of a lot.

Staci Nettles (I was blessed with having her in three classes!) kicked my foot under the desk and handed me a green spiral notebook. I put it on my lap and opened it. *Slam Book*. There were all kinds of questions and answers. Someone had written, *Who ate a whole lasagna and barfed it up on their living room floor?* and someone had answered, *Lily Chin smells like vomit.* Someone else had written, *Lily's chin smells like vomit.* And there was this one: *Lily Chin's eyes pop out of her head because she makes herself throw up so much.* It was so mean that I felt like throwing up, myself. I saw one question that read, *Who is GAY?* and next to it about five people had written about Bobby Castillo. *Bobby Castillo is a fag. Bobby Castillo takes it in the . . .* That sort of thing.

Bobby Castillo was the most beautiful boy in school. I had a crush on him from the first second I saw him, and everyone else, boys and girls, probably did, too. He had tumbling brown curls, perfect amber skin, white teeth, and almond-shaped cat eyes like green, cut glass. They're just jealous, I thought. And scared of their own feelings.

In the book there was also plenty of stuff about Mr. Gibbous, who tended to get very excited and upset when we wouldn't listen. *Is that a banana in Mr. Monkey's pocket or is he just glad to see us?* it said. I slammed the book closed and held it in my lap. I wanted to rip it to shreds, burn it, but I didn't. I just sat there. I was too scared. Finally, when the bell rang I walked past the trash can. And threw that slam book inside.

I went into the bathroom and looked at myself in the mirror. My face was all swollen from my sunburn and my eyes were bloodshot from chlorine and getting to sleep too late the night before. My hair was a mess and I wanted to take a scissors and chop it off right there. My arms and legs were like twigs, my shoulders hunched, and then there was the problem of my non-existent breasts. I wondered what people had written about me in the slam book, or what they were going to write. I wondered if they would find out that my dad had left and my mom drank too much and that they had been screaming at each other so that everyone in our building could see and hear.

The girl in the mirror wasn't who I wanted to be and her life wasn't the one I wanted to have.

Whose father left? the slam book would read.

Louise's father left. Weetzie's would never really leave. Would he?

But he had left. This is what happened the day before the slam book:

There was a smog alert at school and we missed PE. That part of it was okay—I hated having to change into those pilling, striped T-shirts and polyester shorts in front of the girls with breasts and I was embarrassed by my weak arms that couldn't do pull-ups and my skinny legs that couldn't get me around the track as fast as the jock girls. But the smog was worse. Maybe the smog was part of the poison, I don't know. The smog and the martinis, in their icy green glasses, not to mention my dad's other "substances" as my mom called them, whatever they were exactly.

I came home from school. I was wearing Kork-Ease beige suede-and-leather platform sandals but they weren't the cool, high kind that Staci Nettles had. They were the little mini versions that the unpopular girls wore. I also had on hip-hugger jeans and a blouse I had made from old embroidered linen handkerchiefs stitched together. I had blow-dried my long brown hair with a round brush to make wings on either side of my face. Even though it is thin, it felt really hot and sticky on my neck that day.

I ran inside. My mom was sitting in front of the TV, as usual. Her dark roots were eating up the blonde hair and she had on her worn-out pink bathrobe. It was the one she'd stolen from the hotel where she and my dad went on their honeymoon. I said hi and she looked up at me with glassy eyes.

"Did Charlie call yet?" I asked her. We hadn't seen him for a couple of days. That happened every so often but this time I was more worried about it than usual because the last fight had been so bad.

She shook her head. I could tell by the look on her

face that I shouldn't ask any more questions.

I went into my room, put on my bathing suit, which was a two-piece that sagged at the chest and around the butt and was infinitely less sexy than the macramé string bikini I really wanted, and grabbed my mom's *Vogue* magazine and a bottle of Bain de Soleil. On my way to the pool I got a can of Tab, sleek and sweaty with cold. The sun was shining on the water, making long, bright squiggles on the blue. I lay on the plastic lounge chair and slathered myself with the suntan lotion. I drank my Tab. It tasted like sweet liquid metal. I closed my eyes and the sun on the water made sparkling patterns through my eyelids. The sun was like a drug. It burned the sad feeling out of my bones, the feeling that came when I thought of my parents fighting, my dad leaving for days at a time, the empty bottles of alcohol strewn around the apartment. I turned over on my stomach and fell asleep.

I woke up at sunset with my skin tingling. I knew I was burned—I'd be the color of the sky. The air was getting cool so I wrapped up in a towel and went back upstairs. My mom was still in front of the TV. I heated up some frozen mac and cheese for us and sat next to her while we watched *Happy Days* and *Welcome Back, Kotter.* The raised pile of the cheap blue velveteen couch irritated my burned legs but I distracted myself from thinking about that or about my dad by listening to canned sitcom laughter and imagining riding on the back of the Fonz's motorcycle.

"Please get me another gin and tonic," my mom said, holding out her glass regally without looking at me.

I went to the bar and made her drink, minus the gin.

"And what is this, Louise?" She called me Louise when she was mad.

"My name isn't Louise," I said. "And it's tonic, Mom."

"I didn't ask for this." She glared at me and tapped fake red fingernails on the glass. "Louise."

"I don't want you to drink so much," I said.

"Stop telling me what I can and cannot do. You are not the parent."

But the thing was, neither was she. She didn't act like one anyway. I wanted a mom who would act like one, who would ask me how my day was and smooth the hair out of my eyes and rub sunscreen on my shoulders with cool hands.

The walls of my room were painted teeth-grinding yellow. There were beanbag chairs and the waterbed had beaded curtains hanging around it. My mom had put up a few posters of David Cassidy and Bobby

Sherman with their baby faces and shaggy hair and skinny chests but I wasn't that into them. I guess she wanted me to seem like a normal teenager in case anyone came over—she had done all this as a surprise the summer before I started junior high. But I missed my peony-pink room at the canyon cottage where we had lived before it burned down.

I was at home with my mom when the electric wires sparked and the sparks caught a tree by the front door on fire. It turned out that the squirrels had eaten through the wire insulations.

"Squirrels love to sharpen their teeth on those," the firemen said later.

My mom picked me up, still clutching the book she was reading to me, and we ran outside. I screamed and cried for my plush bear, Mink, and my doll Petal Bug as if they were my children. My mom handed me to a neighbor and ran back in. She grabbed Mink and Petal Bug and brought them out to me. By the time the firemen got there, flames were leaping out of the windows, the air was black with ash, and almost everything inside was gone.

My mom had been brave that day. Strong and brave and sober. But she started to drink when we moved to the Starlight Condominiums where we live now.

I still have Mink and Petal Bug—even though I am

thirteen I actually still sleep with them at night and hide them under the bed in the day in case my mom gets drunk and goes on one of her rare cleaning sprees in which she throws out everything in sight. I still have the book we'd rescued, too.

The Lonely Doll has a pink-and-white-gingham-checked cover and black-and-white photos of a doll named Edith and the father teddy bear and baby bear she lives with. Edith reminds me of a devious Goldilocks who had gotten her secret wish—to take Mama Bear's place. Edith and Baby Bear always get into mischief and Father Bear has to discipline them in a stern but loving way. As a kid I was a little disturbed, but also intrigued, by the way he put Edith over his knee and spanked her.

I knew I was way too old for this book now but I read it in secret when I needed comforting. Sometimes I pretended to be Edith, even with the spankings. I never wanted to end up alone.

That night I took a cool shower, put lotion on my sunburn, and lay down on my sloshy bed and read *The Lonely Doll* until I passed out, holding on tight to Mink and Petal Bug.

The shouting was so loud it woke me. They had been shouting at each other a lot but this time their voices sounded a little different. I opened the sliding-glass door and went out on the balcony. They were standing by the pool under the lights, like they were on a stage for everyone to see. I don't remember exactly what they said and it doesn't matter. My mom had a drink in her hand and even from the balcony in the night I could see that she was shaking in her pink robe. I could smell chlorine, so strongly that it felt like I had swallowed some pool water. I wanted to dive into the pool from the balcony where I stood, dive down into the water where I couldn't hear them shouting at each other, just like our goldfish, Garbo, immune in her bowl with the porcelain mermaid and the tiny castle.

Then I saw my mom throw her drink into my dad's face. He staggered back and reached out and grabbed her by the wrists. He took the glass out of her hand and threw the rest of the drink back at her. I'd seen them fight before but they had never gotten physical with each other like that.

My mom teetered on her gold mules. For a moment, everything was still. You could only hear the pool cleaner chugging and spitting, the water gurgling. Then my dad let go of my mom and turned and walked away. I watched her standing there, watching him go. She didn't even scream anymore. She looked very small from above.

It felt like a long time passed. I heard my father's engine start and his yellow Thunderbird drive away. My chest felt numb, as if I'd just had a shot of novocaine in my heart. And then I watched my mother stagger backward and fall into the pool.

I ran back through the condo and out and down the stairs screaming for help and when I got to the pool I saw a boy in the water with my mother. I dove in, too. The water churned around us, stinging my eyes and nostrils with chlorine and sloshing into my mouth. I reached for my mom but I was suddenly too weak, as if all the life in me was being sucked down the drain at the bottom of the pool. That was when I felt arms lifting me up and out.

Then we were all on the side of the pool and the boy shouted up to the surrounding buildings: "Call 911!"

He was skinny and tan with very strong-looking arms and longish blonde hair that dripped over his face. He bent over my mom and pressed on her chest and water came out of her mouth. I'd learned CPR in camp when I was a little kid, practicing blowing into the mouths of baby dolls, but I couldn't remember anything. But the boy knew what he was doing because he leaned over and breathed into her mouth and I saw her eyelids flutter and she opened her eyes.

In that moment a weird thing happened—instead of the boy, I saw Charlie there, bending over my mom, blowing life into her. For a second they were one person, the mystery boy and my dad. All the love I felt for my father, all the love that had gotten scattered in the wind when I saw Charlie leave, was attaching to the boy like glitter attaches to glue when you sprinkle it on your art project.

He looked at me with his blue eyes for just one second but the gaze dropped so deeply into me, like a stone in water—rings and rings. Then he and Charlie were both gone, vanished, like they had never been there at all.

By the time the paramedics came I had my mother sitting up, wrapped in a towel. The paramedics checked her out and said she was okay and then they left, too. I watched their strong shoulders being swallowed up by the nighttime. I wanted something more from them—some reassuring look or smile, but they had only seemed bored and tired as if they saw this thing all the time. It had only happened once to me and I never wanted it to happen again.

I brought my mom upstairs and put her to bed under the baby-blue satin quilt. I gently combed her hair away from her face. It felt like straw in my hands from all the bleach, disintegrating at the ends. I wiped off her face with a towel and smoothed lotion onto her legs and feet. She started to doze off. I was sitting next to her, holding her hand when she opened her eyes and looked at me.

"Why?" she said. "Why didn't you just let me go?"

"Mom!" I hugged her but she was rigid in my arms. We still smelled like chlorine. The odor made me nauseous. "Brandy-Lynn!" I said. "I need to talk to Dad."

"Never tell anyone!" She was shouting now. "Never tell anyone about this. Ever. Especially him."

I won't tell him. But I have to tell someone. I have to at least write it down.

I don't know what happened between my parents. I know that my mom was drinking too much and my dad was "abusing substances," as my mom called it. I know there were money problems. But I don't know the really deep reasons, the reasons why love can turn into screaming and hate. Or at least something that looks like hate, especially to a thirteen-year-old.

I know that my mom and dad loved each other once. When my dad was successful with the monster and sci-fi movies, and even after he wasn't, when we lived in that little cottage in the canyon. It had a shingled roof and thick creamy walls and wooden floors that my mom polished with lemon oil soap until they shone. There were big windows with leaded glass panes and a garden full of roses and day lilies. There was a little fishpond and a jacaranda tree and a winding moss-covered path that led nowhere. My dad played the piano with my bare baby feet, dangling me above the keys as I danced out a tune. My mom made pot roasts and baked potatoes for dinner. She wore a flowered apron and her high heels. We all ate together every night. There was one small black-and-white TV but we hardly ever watched it. When it broke, my dad repaired the antenna with wire hangers. The sun shone at a low angle through the leaded glass windows and across the shiny wooden floors, making the dust motes shine like fairies. There was a lemon tree outside my bedroom window and it was covered with pink and white blossoms and yellow lemons, so bright they glowed in the dark. My parents played jazz and rock and roll on the stereo. They played The Beatles a lot. I used to dance to The Beatles for them in the living room while my dad shone a desk lamp on me like a spotlight. I'd make costumes out of things I'd found in the dress-up box. My mom always saved her old dresses, even when they were ripped or out of style, so I had quite a collection to choose from. She had all these satiny cocktail things and lace suits and sequined or bead-covered cashmere sweaters and leopard-print hats and gloves and spike-heeled pumps with pointed toes. My mother had been a starlet before I was born. She met my dad when she landed a role in his movie *Planet of the Mummy Men*. She was so beautiful then, staring up at my dad in almost every single photograph, a halo of light around her pale hair, as she reclined on the beach with her Betty Grable legs stretched out in front of her, sitting at a nightclub in a pink cocktail dress, smiling over her shoulder, her eyes sparkling like diamonds so that she didn't need jewelry. When I saw her on screen the first time, I thought she actually looked like Marilyn Monroe, who she was always talking about. She had wanted to be the next Marilyn. When she gave birth to me on the day Marilyn died, she thought it was a sign. A sign of what, I'm not sure. That she would go back to her career? That I would be an actress? That I was Marilyn reincarnated? That I was doomed because I was born on one of the saddest days of my mom's life, and everybody else's, too, for that matter?

I love how sad Marilyn's eyes look, even when she is smiling. I love her body that just looks like it wants to give itself to everyone like a present. I love her skin and hair like an angel's. (I always talk about her in the present tense like she didn't die—who else do you do that with?) She was married to a famous baseball player and a famous, brilliant writer who looked like my dad. I love that. And I love how funny and smart she is and how she makes people fall in love with her with just one look.

They say Marilyn's hand was outstretched to the phone when they found her naked on her bed in her apartment in Brentwood. I don't think she really wanted to die. But you never know.

My mom almost died that night by the pool. She wanted to, even though she still had me. Marilyn didn't have any kids at all. I used to wish she were my mom— maybe I could have saved her life, too.

But it wasn't me who rescued my mother. It was the boy. I wanted to find him again and thank him.

THE GIRL
ON THE STAIR

*A*fter school that day, I went from door to door in our building, saying I was doing a project for school on statistics and that I had to find out exactly how many men, women, boys, and girls lived in each unit. I knew most of the neighbors but I kept hoping someone I didn't know, someone who had just moved in, would say they had a son or a brother, or, even better, that the angel boy would answer the door, but there was no sign of him. I wondered if I had made him up. But

I could remember his thin, muscled arms and the pale color of his hair and the sharp line of his cheekbones. Also his pale blue eyes, the color of the pool at night. He reminded me of the pop stars my mom had put up on the walls of my room. They all looked a little like girls and that made you like them because they seemed sweet and soft and familiar as well as unfamiliar at the same time. But the boy was much better than the one-dimensional magazine cutouts on my walls. His skin was warm and wet when he dove into my life. Thinking about him made my body pound with adrenalin, made me feel alive with blood. I felt as real as I'd ever felt, so he must be real, too, I reasoned. At least I thought so.

I didn't find the boy. This is what I found:

Unit 1: Tom "Sunshine" Abernathy (33), Marilyn Monroe impersonator. I'd met him before. He let me try on his wig once.

Unit 2: Uncle Oz (75), retired set designer, currently a collector of antique toys and children's books. When I was younger my mom brought me over there and he read me fairy tales.

Unit 3: Mimi Jones (25), elementary schoolteacher and fashion plate. I liked to spy on her outfits every morning. She wore mini skirts, suede platforms, colored stockings, and false eyelashes and smoked like a very busy chimney.

Unit 4: Candy Red (20???), "professional." She was not very friendly to me and told me I should do a report on someone else's building.

Unit 5: Dori Knight (19) and Elsie Capshaw (19). College girls with retail jobs.

Unit 6: Ben Hoopelson. I have no idea how old he is. He is a mime and won't talk.

Unit 7: Carla St. Clair (27), TV hair and makeup artist. A friend of Mimi Jones.

Unit 8: Arthur (39), Esther (30), Abe (10), and Rebecca (8) Steinberg. Orthodox Jews. Arthur is a teacher. Their apartment smelled like fresh baked bread and simmering meat.

Unit 9: Brandy-Lynn Bat (35), Weetzie Bat (13).

Unit 10: Bob (33) and Nancy (27) Levine, assistant professor and homemaker, lovey-dovey newlyweds. They answered the door with their arms around each other, wearing matching aprons.

Unit 11: Tim (30) and Andrea (29) Shore, movie grip and secretary. They fought almost as much as my mom and dad.

Unit 12: The Mendoza family—Jose (40), Teresa (37), Wendy and Mary (15). A very nice family. The twins went to my school.

Unit 13: ???

The only interesting new person I saw was a tall, lanky lady with a thick accent I didn't recognize, long black hair, and huge eyes that were such a dark shade of blue they were almost purple. Maybe they were just reflecting her pantsuit. She gave me a nasty look and shut the door of Unit 13 on me before I could even ask her anything. There was something vaguely familiar about her but I couldn't place it.

As soon as I got home, all the energy in my body just drained away. There were dirty dishes in the sink and empty bottles everywhere—the trash cans hadn't been emptied and bills were scattered all over the kitchen table. I hated our condo. It was like as soon as my dad stopped making money and we lost the cottage, my mom had to suddenly pretend we were rich and glamorous. She had to decorate with fake golden cupids and baby-blue velveteen and thick shag carpeting. I remembered the simple cottage with the wooden floors and the flowers everywhere. I remembered my mom dancing around in her cotton dresses.

My mom looked like she hadn't gotten out of bed all day. I brought her Brazil nuts and ginger ale and red licorice. I would have tried to cook but I always burned the grilled cheese sandwiches or let the rice bubble over. The only thing I could make was instant mac and cheese but she didn't want that and neither did I. I wished she had taught me to cook when I was littler and she was happy and loved to make dinner but now it was probably too late.

While we watched *Tony Orlando & Dawn*, I stared at Tony's huge mustache and his backup singers' glittery dresses wondering how they could have landed a whole show for themselves based on a song about a yellow ribbon around an oak tree. The music wasn't distracting enough—I thought about my dad and when he was going to call. When the program was over and my mom was asleep, passed out in front of a cop show, I went into my parents' bedroom, into the closet, and I put my face in my dad's shirts and sniffed his tobacco and woodsy-smelling aftershave and wished he would appear inside his suit and hold me and hug me and say that he loved us and would never leave again.

But my dad didn't even call that night.

I tucked my mom in and turned off the TV, wishing that *Cher* was on. There was nothing more beautiful to me than Cher in her sheer dresses with the strategic beading and her belly button showing. And the way she flicked her black Arabian horse mane off her bony shoulder and laughed like she didn't want to show her cute tiny vampire teeth but she couldn't help it and her shiny lips would part and her teeth would show. And her voice would crack. Sometimes she'd be an Indian American with feathers, straddling a horse, and sometimes she'd be a showgirl with feathers. No matter what she wore she was sexy and beautiful but she didn't look like anyone else on TV. I thought about Cher in her feathers because it was better than thinking about my dad and how he hadn't called and because it was easier to wish for a TV show than for the person you loved more than anyone else.

Then I realized that the new woman in our building looked a little like Cher and for some reason that took away the comfort I'd been feeling. Suddenly, even Cher made me sad.

I turned off the lights and went out onto the balcony and looked down at the pool. I remembered the boy crouching over my mother, his tense shoulders and his strong hands. Maybe he would come back? I put on my sweatshirt over my pajamas, pushed my bare feet into my Vans, and left the apartment.

I went downstairs and sat by the pool and stared at the ghostly blue water and thought about my dad. Was he gone forever? Would he call me? Would he come back? He'd gone away before, on a pretty regular basis, to do some writing or to see his sister, Goldy, in New York or after fights with my mom, but there had never been a fight like this. When he went away, he would always leave me a bottle of his aftershave to use when he was gone so that I would remember him. He also let me wear his shirts. The shirts smelled like cigarettes and the aftershave and if I wore one and closed my eyes and rubbed a piece of sandpaper, as scratchy and granular as his chin, it was like he was there with me.

I realized that I could go get one of my dad's shirts and wear the aftershave now—he hadn't had time to get anything when he left. But I knew it would upset my mom. I'd have to wear the shirt at night while I slept or sneak out in it in the morning. Plus, I didn't know if I could stand wearing that shirt. It would make me too sad, that smoky, leafy, cinnamon-tinged smell.

I was lying on a lounge chair and the plastic slats were cutting into my skin through my thin pajamas. I shifted my weight and looked up at the sky. You couldn't see any stars. I remember going back east with my dad, how he showed me the stars in upstate New York, above this old farmhouse with a creek where Goldy lived, and I was so surprised how many there were. In L.A. the stars look weak and forlorn like the people who come here to be famous and end up working as waiters. Except they are beautiful, too. Like this really cute guy who worked at the Great American Food & Beverage Company on Santa Monica Boulevard. My parents took me there on my twelfth birthday and the cute waiter sang me Cat Stevens songs and brought me a Cobb salad and a piece of birthday cake. And there were the cute, old waitresses at Du-Par's in the Valley who had probably been starlets once. They wore little, ruffled aprons and pink dresses and squeaky orthopedic shoes and they all reminded me not only of the faded stars in the sky but also of the pretty whipped-cream-covered pies reflected in tilted mirrors along the very top of the walls still hoping to be discovered, if only for a tiny part in a pie commercial.

All these thoughts made me hungry and I was getting sleepy so I decided to go back in because it didn't seem as if the boy was going to come. I could have jumped into the pool and pretended to be drowning but that seemed too dramatic so I got up and started toward the stairs.

I was standing at the bottom of the staircase going up to our unit when I heard this cackling laughter. It had a shockingly hollow sound.

There was a girl about my age sitting at my front door.

She was thin and pale with long, black hair that hung almost to her waist, and large, tilted eyes that looked like the eyes of the woman in number 13. The girl was wearing a childlike, too-small dress with puffed sleeves and a smocked bodice that came to just below where her fairly large (at least compared to mine) breasts were. She also had on bobby socks and old-fashioned white saddle shoes. Her lips were bright red with lipstick.

"You can't go home again," she told me sternly. "Don't even try it. Home is gone forever." Then she laughed that hollow doll cackle.

I backed away and started running. I ran and ran into the night. It was dark and cold and empty, without even the comfort of a moon anywhere in sight, let alone stars. I thought about the cute waiter who would probably never get a record deal and how the feet of the waitresses at Du-Par's must hurt them a lot.

A man in a fancy, white Mercedes pulled up beside me, leaning out the window, and I ran faster, my heart calling uselessly for help inside me.

All I could make out clearly were his eyes, catching a reflection of the streetlights beneath the white turban he wore—they looked like they had seen everything there was to see.

"You must not be afraid," he told me, then reached

his hand out the window and tossed something onto the sidewalk before he sped away.

I stopped where I stood, breathing hard, looking at the something—it was a shiny silver envelope.

You must not be afraid.

The man in the car, whoever he was, was right. I'd already lost what was most important to me—my dad. I didn't have anything to be afraid of except that he might not come back. I didn't have anything to care about and sometimes that makes you brave.

I picked up the envelope and opened it. There was a note inside. I unfolded it and a cascade of tiny glittery bits fell out. The words were written in cutout letters like a ransom note:

Mirror mirror on the wall, you're Factor's fairest of them all.

What the heck? Fairest of them all? Factor's? I tucked the note in my pocket and walked home. Some of the glitter had clung to my arms like shiny freckles.

When I got back, determined to stand my ground against the cackling girl, she—just like the mysterious boy—was gone, if she had ever been there at all. In a way I was relieved: even with the encouraging words I wasn't brave enough to stand up to her anyway. Not yet.

That night I lay in bed staring at the note. What did it mean? It seemed like a clue of some sort but I had no idea how to read it. I wasn't anybody's fairest and who was Factor anyway? I tucked the note inside my pink ballerina music box and closed my eyes, hoping I'd dream about Charlie that night.

When my dad used to get upset and I asked him why, he didn't talk too much about my mom. He usually blamed Los Angeles.

He said, "Once there at least was noir and sorcerers and cults and jazz and poetry and citrus orchards, Marilyn Monroe and Charlie Chaplin. Now there are just cars and freeways and vapid teenagers who don't even know what noir means. And the music! No one has heard of the Stooges or the Velvet Underground. The singer/songwriters lock themselves up in their canyon mansions wishing for the sixties to come back. I'm sick of the heat. I'm sick of the lack of culture. I have to get out. Someday I'm moving back to N.Y.C."

What he didn't say was L.A. had something else, something that didn't exist in New York City.

L.A. had his daughter, Weetzie. L.A. had me. In a way, L.A. *was* me. I hadn't known anything else and I didn't think I ever would.

Even with the smog alerts, L.A. had never seemed that bad to me. I liked the light. It was always filtered by smog but I didn't think about that. It was dull and golden. My dad said it made people lazy and passive, that light. It lulled you into a stupor. It made you dumb as a pink plastic flamingo, my dad said.

But there was Hollywood Boulevard, starred with the names of my idols. There was the Chinese Theater like a magic pagoda. There was the Sunset Strip winding beneath the giant billboards and lined with places like Tower Records, where I liked to find all the scariest or sexiest album covers in the bins. Along the Strip were restaurants like The Source and Carney's and Butterfield's. The Source was an old shack of a hippie place with wood-paneled walls and an outdoor patio. They served veggie burgers and sprouts and hibiscus lemonade. Carney's was a hot-dog place inside an old train car. Butterfield's was a sunken garden at the bottom of the stairs, like someone's run-down mansion where you could have elegant brunches with quiche, fresh fruit, and champagne among lacy trees. There was Jerry Pillar's, where you could get really cheap designer clothes—there were just rooms and rooms stuffed with piles of crazy jeans and embroidered T-shirts and racks of dresses and shelves of boxes filled with platform sandals and high-heeled suede boots.

And L.A. wasn't only a city. There were canyons and mountains and wonderful parks. On weekends we went to Ferndell in Griffith Park and I played in the shallow water that trickled among rocks down the side of the green hill. The lush plants made a canopy and I felt like I was exploring secret islands. We rode the carousel on top of the hill. The paint was peeling and the colors faded on the horses and murals. The calliope had a haunting sound as I went around and around, up and down, trying to catch sight of myself in the mirrors. Next were the pony rides where my pony would always stop on the dusty track and I refused to hit him with the whip. My dad had to come and lift me off when I started to cry. At Travel Town on the other side of the park we explored the old trains parked on the deserted tracks and rode the miniature one that went around two times while the conductor in the striped hat and overalls rang the bell. The little train passed an even tinier group of buildings half hidden in the grass. I wondered, at the time, if elves lived there.

L.A. had the beach! When I was younger we used

to go to Malibu sometimes, to visit Irv Feingold, the producer my dad had worked with. Irv and his wife, Edie, lived in a big, glass and redwood house right on the sand. I thought at the time that the ocean was the best backyard anyone could ever have—so vast and alive and musical, always changing colors, always singing different songs. We ate little pieces of raw fish and candied ginger and my parents had cocktails and wine. We sat out on the deck watching the waves break and then shiver up the sand. I went down the wooden staircase to the beach and chased gulls and dug for sand crabs. Once I was stung by a jellyfish and the pain felt just like that thing looked—gelatinous and cold and veined with hurt. Once a crab caught hold of my toe and wouldn't let go. I felt the little pincers and I couldn't shake them off. My dad had to do it for me. It still hurt and he rinsed off my foot in the outdoor showers and took me back out to play in the water. He wore shorts and kept his shirt on. His skin looked very white—he wasn't used to the sun. My mom spent the whole time lying on a chaise lounge on the deck working on her tan. She told me that without a tan her skin looked green—I wondered if I looked green to her so I started tanning, too. We used Johnson's baby oil and then a few years later we switched to Bain de Soleil, which smelled like coconuts and was supposed to be better for you. When I came back up from the beach, there were thick, black tar stains on my feet. We needed to clean them off with rubbing alcohol in the producer's glamorous bathroom with the sunken pink marble tub. The producer's wife, Edie, wore hand-painted silk chiffon dresses with handkerchief hems. She was much younger than he was and my mom got really agitated around her, fussing with her hair and reapplying lipstick all the time. We drove home from the producer's house late at night and sometimes I think my dad had too much to drink but I still slept peacefully in the car, lulled by the dark and the cooling heat on my shoulders and the sound of my parents' voices gently arguing and the sound of the radio.

I loved the radio. I would lie in the dark with my ear to the speaker listening to the popular songs. There was a song I liked called "Seasons in the Sun." I knew it was cheesy, especially compared to the "serious" music my dad liked but I liked it anyway. It was about a boy who was dying, saying good-bye to the girl he loved. It made me cry. I closed my eyes and saw a boy and a girl running on the beach. The light was gold and dangerous. The boy was going to die. It was Los Angeles light.

The gentle arguing escalated to screams of broken glass. We hadn't been to the private beach in Malibu in a while. I heard Edie, the young wife in hand-painted silk chiffon, had left Irv, the producer. The boy in the song was probably dead.

My dad was gone.

You must not be afraid, the man in the Mercedes had said.

But I always kind of was.

WINTERISH

The next day there was a green spiral notebook on my desk in Miss Spinner's class. My heart started pounding so hard I thought it would slam through my chest. The notebook turned out to only be someone's English journal, left behind from the last class, but after that, everywhere I looked I thought I saw that slam book following me around. I wondered what they were going to write about me. It made me sweat no matter how much antiperspirant I used. L.A. didn't seem beautiful to me anymore. The air was always hot like the city was on fire.

When I came home from school, three red dogs were sitting in front of our door. They were sitting so close together that they looked like one dog with three heads. I vaguely remembered a story my dad had told me about a three-headed dog that guarded the gates of hell. My mom was always getting mad at my dad for telling me scary stories but I liked them. And I wasn't usually scared of dogs—I loved dogs. I walked the ones in the neighborhood to make extra money and I loved them all. The little, snippety ones and the shy, fat ones and the strong, proud ones. I begged my parents for a puppy all the time. But now I was afraid.

The dogs growled at me and licked their chops. They had sharp ears and teeth and angry curling tails. I backed away. That was when I heard the cackling sound. It was the girl again. She was standing behind me with her arms crossed over her chest. She wore the same childish dress and shoes.

"What's wrong?" she said in that voice like an angry bird's. "Don't you like my chow chows?" The dogs growled and she clicked her tongue at them.

"Your dogs are in front of my door," I said.

"Oh, really? Just like I was the other night. How funny." She began to laugh.

"Please move them."

"Sure!" She bent over and clapped her hands. "Come on, boys," she said. "Go get her!"

The dogs tensed, and sniffed the air, then leaped up and tore down the stairs toward me. I took my roller skates off my shoulder and stood ready to hurl them at the vicious red fur faces. I don't remember anything more about that moment except the sound of a whistle behind me. The dogs stopped and put their heads down, began to whimper.

The boy, the one from the pool, was standing there.

"Anna," he said. "What the hell are you doing? Get them out of here!"

The girl stared at him and opened her mouth like she was going to say something, but he raised his hand—his pale blue eyes were a command. She called the dogs and huffed off daintily with her nose and butt in the air.

I sat down on the bottom of my steps and rubbed the sides of my face. I was too freaked out to even be happy to see Angel Boy.

"What was that?" I asked.

He flipped his skateboard up with one toe and caught it. "Are you okay?"

"Who are you? And why are you always here when I need you?"

He shrugged. "You sure do need me a lot," he said. Then he added: "He was right."

Before I could say anything else, he had skated away over the pavement, swiveling his hips slightly to steer the board. I didn't even try to run after him, though I wanted to. Everything was just too weird.

"Mom," I said out loud, but barely. "I need help. I need you." I knew she couldn't hear me and that she probably wouldn't come even if she could. "Mom? Dad?"

Who was the boy? He had rescued me two times. He knew the girl, and the dogs. He seemed to know me, too. Maybe he really was my guardian angel. I wished he had stayed long enough for me to talk to him, although I wouldn't have really known what to say. He was so cute that after I recovered from the shock of what had happened I would probably have started mumbling or stuttering and made a fool out of myself.

All I wanted was for Charlie to call. I had no idea how to reach him. The only real friend he had was Irv Feingold and I didn't have his phone number. Besides, what would I say—*Have you seen my daddy*? And he probably didn't want to think about people leaving after what happened with Edie.

Actually, I didn't just want Charlie to call—I wanted him to drive up in the battered yellow T-bird and take me away. We would drive across the country, all the way to the East Coast. We would live in a tiny apartment in Manhattan and I would go to school there. I wouldn't miss the sun. I wouldn't miss the pink sky. I wouldn't miss the palm trees or the diamonds in the pavement. I would see beauty again, everywhere I looked. I would paint the walls of my room pink and I'd paint the floor black with silver sparkles. My dad would take me to the Metropolitan Museum to see the huge Buddhas and the indoor pyramid and the van Goghs. I'd learn about all the weird, dark music that he had told me about. The Velvet Underground and the Stooges. I'd be someone else. No one would ever call me Louise again.

I trudged upstairs, like I had huge boots on my feet instead of the shortest version of lightweight cork platform sandals, and threw down my backpack. My mom was watching TV.

"Did you hear the dogs?" I asked her, but she didn't answer so I asked again.

"Dogs? What dogs? There aren't any dogs in this building."

"Now there are," I said. "Do you know about any

new people who moved in?"

My mom pulled her bathrobe over her pilling, pale yellow nylon negligee. She had streaks of mascara on her cheeks and her face looked bloated. Her voice sounded muffled, cottony. "What?"

"There was a weird girl with three dogs. She tried to sic them on me. This boy stopped them."

"There aren't any new people here."

"In Unit Thirteen."

"This building doesn't have a thirteen. Bad luck." She turned back to the TV. "And if it did, no one would live in it."

"He was the boy that saved you," I said but she wasn't listening. She had turned the TV sound up louder and was staring at the screen as if she could disappear inside if she stared hard enough.

Then the phone rang and we both jumped. She got it before I could.

"Hello? Hello?"

She slammed the receiver down.

"Who was that?" I asked.

"They hung up. Wrong number probably."

School was not where I wanted to be either but it was better than home. Or was it? There weren't any chow dogs after me but there was Staci Nettles and she was about as bad.

"Hey," she said. She and her friends, Marci Torn and Kelli Glass, were standing in front of me as I sat on the front steps putting on my skates. They flipped their hair in perfect unison. I noticed my neighbors, the twins Mary and Wendy Mendoza, were watching from a little distance away.

"Hi, Staci."

"I saw you throw the slam book away."

I could hardly tie my laces under her stare.

"We could have gotten busted. Luckily, Marci fished it out or you would have been in deep shit."

I realized I was holding my breath. Certain people can smell fear the way dogs do.

"I strongly suggest you never do anything like that again," Staci told me. "Stand up."

"What?" I said.

"Stand up." Marci and Kelli took me by the shoulders and lifted me into position, held me there.

Then Staci stretched her gum out over her tongue and blew a giant pink bubble in my face.

I rocked unsteadily backward on my wheels, caught myself. Staci took the wad of gum out of her mouth, examined it thoughtfully, and stuck it in my hair.

The hair that I had finally, painstakingly grown out of its pixie cut. The hair that, though thinner and less shiny than Staci's, Marci's, or Kelli's, still rendered me less vulnerable to the cruelty of junior high. Or so I thought. Hair was power. Think of Marilyn. Think of Elizabeth Taylor. Think of Bette Davis. They were defined by their hair.

The blood rushed to my face and I reached to feel the sticky wad of saliva-soaked putty matting together the thin strands.

Wendy and Mary Mendoza shook their heads at Staci. Then they waved their hands in the air in an odd gesture that looked as if they were summoning someone.

"Not again," I heard a voice say with a sigh.

Staci, Marci, Kelli, and I turned around—there was a boy standing there, watching us. Mary and Wendy were gone.

"Are you getting into trouble again?" the boy asked.

The girls' mouths hung open as they looked from him to me, and back again. Weetzie knew this guy? The cutest boy ever? An older boy?

I didn't want him to see me like this. Sweaty and upset and with gum in my hair. Cornered by the prettiest, meanest girl in my grade. Why was he here? "I don't need your help."

Staci, Marci, and Kelli snickered. The boy moved closer to me. "You need to leave her alone."

"Come on, Weetzie," he said, taking my hand, which immediately started to sweat. "I've got the Bug. I'll give you a ride."

I went with him shakily on my skates and when we got to the yellow VW with the surfboard on top I leaned against the side for support. He opened the passenger door for me.

"They're still watching," he said. "Do you want to get in?"

"I don't know you," I replied. "You could be anyone, anyone at all." When I was nervous or upset I sometimes spoke like someone out of an old movie.

He squinted at me. He was wearing a pale blue cotton T-shirt the color of his eyes and off-white painter's pants with the loop on the side for the paintbrush.

"My name is Winter," he said.

"How do you know my name?"

"I know Charlie." He glanced over at the girls behind us. "They're still watching."

I got in the car. He knew Charlie. He knew my dad.

I was driving away from school in a yellow VW Bug with the cutest boy I'd ever seen up this close. *I know*

Charlie, he'd said.

"You okay?" he asked me, not looking over.

"Did you say your name is Winter?"

"Yeah."

"Last name?"

"First name. My last name's much weirder."

"There's no winter in L.A." I didn't mean to be rude but another thing I did when I was nervous was to chatter randomly.

"I know. I guess just winterish. I was born in late December."

I fingered the wad of gum in my hair. I wanted to tear it out. I wanted to take a shower and rinse away all of Staci's spit from my body. I wish I had worn something cute. I had on my red Dittos from last year and they were a little too short in the leg and pulled at the crotch. Red wasn't even my color. But since my dad left I just wore whatever I could grab in the morning and mostly it didn't matter—there wasn't anyone I wanted to impress anymore.

"Besides, with a glass castle name like yours I wouldn't be throwing stones." He grinned goodnaturedly. "Weetzie? *Bat?*"

"How do you know Charlie?" I asked him. He

punched a cassette into the car stereo. It was a woman's voice—harsh but somehow seductive—it made me want to hear more.

"You call him Charlie?"

"I just started when I was little. I had this huge crush on Charlie Chaplin and it made me think of him when I said it. It made us feel closer, too, I think. Like our special language. Charlie and Weetzie instead of Daddy and Louise." Why had I told him so much? Sometimes I just babbled on.

"Louise?"

"You didn't answer my question."

I wasn't sure if he was going to. Finally, he said, "When he left he asked if I'd look out for you."

"What does that mean?" I asked. So much for my guardian angel theory. Or maybe not? "That doesn't tell me anything."

"I wasn't supposed to tell you." He turned onto our street. It was that September late afternoon time when the light slants through the leaves casting purplish-blue shadows and the air is just beginning to crackle with the smell of autumn. "Don't mention me to him."

I closed my eyes and pushed my head back against the headrest. Some of the stuffing was coming out of the seat underneath me. The car smelled musty, like sawdust. The engine rumbled in the back. Bugs were weird, really, like little animals. There used to be this one that drove around town with eyelashes attached over the headlights.

"Well, now you have to. Tell me, I mean."

"I didn't think I'd have to help you so many times," he said. "I mean, it's only been a few days since he left, right? I didn't think I'd ever even have to meet you."

"Oh, great, thanks."

He parked the car and turned to look at me. I sat frozen in profile, the gum in my lank hair. What did he see when he looked at me? What did anyone see? Not someone lovable enough to keep her father from leaving.

I flashed back to a year before, riding on a bus in San Francisco with my dad.

Charlie has taken Weetzie there for her twelfth birthday. They stay in a tiny, lovely Victorian hotel on a steep hill and eat fettuccine at an Italian restaurant. The waiter takes her food away before she is done and she cries— Charlie orders her a whole new plate, fresh and steaming. She is happy but tries not to think about the fact that her mom isn't there with them.

That weekend is the first time she thinks she is in love.

49

On the bus there is a beautiful man, the most beautiful man she has ever seen, tall and thin with sparkling green eyes and golden skin and hair and a gold hoop in his ear. He is holding a bouquet of roses and she can't help thinking he is the one. It sounds silly to someone who doesn't understand but she is devastated by the fact that this man doesn't notice her, even though she could so easily imagine spending the rest of her life with him. She doesn't realize until later that why she was so upset, why she had this fantasy at all, had to do with the fact that her mom isn't there, that they weren't traveling as a family.

Love is so weird.

"I have to go," I said to Winter, and I got out.

"If you didn't keep getting into trouble, this wouldn't have happened," he said, not looking at me, his eyes on the steering wheel.

"I'm not getting myself into trouble! It was that girl with the dogs! You're the one who knows her!"

"And the girls at school?" he said, still staring straight ahead.

"I don't need any more of your help. I'm perfectly fine without you," I told him in my movie star voice as I slammed the door and skated over the cement. When I was upset the rumbling seemed to go right up through my whole body. It was like the streets of Los Angeles talking to me, warning me. A chilly breeze made my whole body shiver with the knowledge that the summer was really over and that autumn wasn't really all that romantic in L.A., just cooler. A cloud passed over the sun, turning the sky dark. I stopped at the bottom of my staircase. Devil Girl wasn't there, the chows weren't there. I felt a mild twinge of disappointment, though. If there was nothing to be protected from, then no one would protect me. If there were no devils, no guardian angels were needed. I took off my skates, draped them over my shoulder, and ran up to my front door and into the baby-blue room, where my reflection watched me in the gold-veined mirror-paneled wall beside the bar, and there was really nothing to protect me from except myself.

Later that night I showered and clipped the huge wad of gum out of my hair. It left a big raggedy space.

Mirror mirror on the wall.

I wasn't anyone fairest. It made me think the note I'd received was a mean-spirited joke. I looked like a freak.

Pixie-cut time again. So much for my wings.

So I clipped and clipped and pretty soon my hair

was short again. At least the hole was gone but the ends were uneven. I couldn't look at it anymore so I went to check on my mom.

She was wearing the same yellow negligee and faded pink bathrobe. There was a time when she wore long, peach silk dressing gowns with puffed sleeves and French lace, strips of sheer creamy chiffon running down the sides. She sometimes pinned gardenias in her hair. They smelled so good I wanted to eat them.

"You have to get out of the house," I told her. "Can I help you pick out an outfit? We could go shopping and out to dinner." That was what to do when we were depressed, after my parents fought and my dad left for a few days. We went to Contempo Casuals boutique and Bullock's department store—there was something comforting about silver escalators ascending skyward, glass walls, eternally poised mannequins, and racks and racks of clothes—and then we ate burgers and fries and drank milk shakes in frosty silver tumblers. Not that I felt like doing any of that anymore.

She looked up at me blearily. The TV was blaring an afternoon talk show. The curtains were drawn closed and the room felt hot and musty. Dust motes sizzled in the sunlight above the shag carpet, like burning fairies.

"Have you eaten?" I asked her.

She raised an empty glass to me.

"Come on, Mom. We'll go out to Norm's or something. I have a little extra cash in my piggy bank. You need a treat."

She shook her head. "I need him."

"I know." I sat down next to her and put my arms around her shoulders. They felt harder than ever, as if she were trying to grow a shell to hide in.

"He'll come back," I said.

She shook her head again, the bleach-burnt hair falling over her tan face. I noticed the chipped red polish on her toes in the gold mules and it shocked me. This was Brandy-Lynn. Polish was never chipped—even in the worst of circumstances polish was perfect.

That was when the phone rang. We both jolted and then sat frozen staring. It rang three times. Then the machine came on. The caller hung up.

Why hadn't I answered it?

"He won't come back," she said. "I thought he loved me and I thought he loved you more. But it isn't true. He can't love you either, not really, to go away like that."

Her eyes filled up with tears and I thought, I am never going to cry about this. No matter what, I am not going to cry. Because what is the point? Crying is really never going to make him come back. Maybe if he sees me smiling, maybe that will work. Maybe if he senses that I am helping people, that I am strong and nice and worth coming back for . . .

Of course, I knew it was impossible but I thought it anyway. That Charlie could see me in the crystal ball in his head and come back.

I was going to take care of myself, I decided. I was not only going to take care of myself, I was going to take care of as many other people as I could. I didn't need that boy named Winter, whoever or whatever he was, to take care of me. I'd show him. I'd show my dad.

That night I washed the dishes that had piled up, vacuumed the carpet, cleaned the bathroom, and did the laundry. I heated up a can of tomato soup for dinner and tried to get my mom to eat it. In the morning I did all the dishes before I went to school.

Are you looking, Daddy?

In Miss Spinner's class I was hunched over my English test, pressing the number two pencil hard into the paper and against the bump that had formed on the side of my middle finger, when I felt a tap on my shoulder. I tried to ignore it. Staci slid the slam book into my lap.

"Nice chop, Louise," she whisper-hissed.

Lily Chin was on the other side of me. I saw a worried look shadow her face and darken her eyes behind her glasses. She had a long, thin neck, braces, and an overdeveloped jaw. At lunchtime she always sat alone, gnawing on those apples as if she both hated them and desired them more than anything in the world.

Suddenly, I felt a tug and the slam book fell off my lap onto the floor. I looked down and saw there was a string attached to it. Staci dropped the end of the string and made a fake-surprised "O" with her mouth.

Miss Spinner looked up.

"What's this?" she said, coming over to my desk.

"It's a slam book, Miss Spinner," said Staci daintily. "Louise has been passing it around."

"Is this true, Louise?"

"Weetzie," I said. "No. I didn't . . ."

Miss Spinner picked up the book and looked at the last page. She put it on my desk, right in front of me. Someone had written in pink pen under *Doggiest Teacher: Miss Spinster has to cross her legs like that because she hasn't ever gotten laid.*

Miss Spinner picked up the pink pen that I kept on my desk. She tapped it on the slam book.

"I didn't write that," I said.

"Please take this piece of fine literature to Mrs.

Musso's office," Miss Spinner said.

"I didn't write it!"

"Go. Now."

Staci smiled at me like I was a piece of sandwich meat and it was 11:45. Lily Chin looked up, alarmed.

I found Lily Chin at lunch. The principal, Mrs. Musso, had let me go when I told her that the pink writing wasn't mine. She made me show her a writing sample. I apologized anyway on the way out.

"Let's not have it happen again," she barked at me, like those chow dogs that had tried to attack. She wore her chow-red hair in a helmet style and mannish skirt suits, her feet jammed into her shoes so her ankles bulged over the top. I wished I could have taken her shopping and to the beauty salon. Actually, I wished I could take myself to the beauty salon and get my hair fixed—maybe I'd go after school with the piggy-bank money my mom hadn't wanted.

Lily Chin and her apple were sitting alone. She was looking at it with an enraptured expression. She was dressed in a baggy sweatshirt, what looked like boy's trousers, and suede Wallabees on her feet. Her hair was in a thin ponytail. I went over and sat down next to her.

"Hi," I said.

She looked at me warily.

I tried to find something to compliment about her clothing. That was the best icebreaker between girls in junior high. Then I noticed her ring—a glassy stone in a silver filigree setting. It was a dark yellow color.

"Cool ring," I said.

A faint smile touched her face like a beam of the sunlight that was sifting through the moving leaves. It revealed the flashing metal of her braces and then was gone. "Thanks."

"Is it a mood ring?"

"Yeah."

I tried to remember what the colors meant. The murky yellow didn't seem to be a good sign.

"You okay?"

She shrugged and examined the ring.

"I think blue is happy?"

"I wouldn't know," she said.

"Can I sit with you?"

She nodded and I sat on the bench next to her. I ate my peanut butter and jelly sandwich and she massacred her apple. I offered her half a frosted Pop-Tart but she looked at it like it might bite back so I quickly returned it to my lunch box. We hardly talked at all but I found it comforting to be sitting with somebody.

When the bell rang I looked at her hand. The ring was milk-blue.

Mirror mirror.

I couldn't give Mrs. Musso a makeover but I could give myself one. After school I went to see Kurt the hairstylist. I brought the last of the dog-walking savings from my piggy bank—my mom didn't seem to care about going out with me anyway.

Kurt had a fancy little salon on Melrose. It was all glass and chrome with pounding music. The singer hollered above the driving guitar. Kurt wore his golden hair in a layered shag cut, dressed in patchwork bell-bottoms, embroidered shirts, and platforms.

"Weetzie!" he cried when I walked in. "What did you do to your hair? You look like creatures nibbled on you."

"Hi, Kurt. A mean girl stuck gum in it."

"Oh those meanies keep getting worse every year. By the time you have kids they'll be shaving each other's hair off while they sleep. Although, you'd actually look pretty bald."

"Thanks a lot."

"Don't get huffy on me. Come sit down."

He shampooed my scalp with deep, sensual strokes,

then spent a long time dramatically ruffling my hair, examining me from every angle. You couldn't talk to him during this point—his eyes would get cartoon-huge and he'd make a zipping motion over his mouth.

When he was done he began to snip meticulously. It was even more forbidden to talk to him at this phase. Then he applied mousse as if it were whipped cream on a banana split and blow-dried my hair with sweeping motions, tossing his own gilt-highlighted mane back and forth and eyeing himself in the mirror. I could talk then.

"What's the music?"

"The New York Dolls. Music and fashion icons. You like?"

"Yeah. It sounds cool. My dad played them for me before, I think."

"What a little rocker he is. I'm going to get hold of him one of these days. That barbershop doesn't do him justice. How is he?"

Charlie had taken me to get my hair cut once. Kurt wanted to get his hands on his hair but my dad hurried off to get coffee and picked me up in front when it was over.

I shrugged. "I haven't heard from him in days."

"What? Where'd he go?"

"I have no idea."

"You need to find him! Tell him to get his butt right back here now!"

"He and my mom got in a fight."

"Brandy-Lynn!" he scolded. "Why doesn't she come in and have her roots done? I'll have a little talk with her."

"It's too late, I think," I said. "She's a mess."

Kurt fussed over my hair, applying hair spray with sweeping movements like he was an insect doing some kind of mating dance. "Well, maybe she'll come see me when she sees how great you look. Ready to go blonde, Weetz-ala?"

"Not today," I told him. "I don't have the cash. Plus, my mom would kill me."

He ignored the second reason because we both knew my mom wouldn't really care—she was too drunk all the time. "It just takes a bottle of bleach and a sink to do it yourself, lover. Now go get those meanies for me!"

On my way out he yelled after me, "Oh, and remember to be nice to *you*! Take Weetzie on a fabulous date. It's good practice."

That night I sat at my mom's sewing machine holding a dress she'd made for me when I was ten. I wanted to keep the dress exactly the way it was, to remind me of my childhood when she made my clothes, even after we left the cottage, sewing each stitch so lovingly, but I also wanted to cut that dress up, make it into something completely different so I could forget. Plus, I needed something to wear on my date with me! I took a pair of scissors and cut out the purple roses printed on the dress and appliquéd them all over a pair of old jeans. And then I sewed one big rose onto the front of a white T-shirt. It was a way to remember and forget at the same time.

The next day at lunch Lily told me I looked cute.

"Thanks. I had to cut my hair."

"And your outfit," she said. I wondered if she hadn't been talking about my hair at all. I touched the back. It suddenly felt way too short.

"If you want you can come over and I'll dress you up."

She laughed. It was the first time I'd seen her do that. Her little teeth showed.

"I'd look dumb," she said, nodding at my purple roses.

"No you wouldn't. Besides, we'd put you together differently."

"Okay," she said. Then she asked, "Why are you being so nice?"

I didn't want to explain about my vow to be nice so that my dad might come back. "You seem cool," I said. "Not like Staci and her friends."

"Yeah. I'm not like them at all."

"Me neither."

"I mean, look at my hair!"

"Look at mine!"

We laughed. Just then, Bobby Castillo walked by. He stopped and smiled at us.

"Oh, my God!" said Lily. "Did you see that? He's so cute."

"His eyelashes go to his toes," I said. "And he's coming over here."

"Hey," said Bobby Castillo with a ferocious grin. "I heard you took the heat for that piece of shit that was going around."

"How'd you hear that?"

"It's all over."

He came and sat next to us. He was so ridiculously foxy that we just stared at him. I felt my cheeks smolder.

"Yeah," I finally said. "Staci tried to make it look like I wrote that thing about Miss Spinner."

"Staci Nettles is a bitch," Bobby Castillo observed

matter-of-factly. "What I don't get is why people don't think being mean sucks. You can't be fat or skinny or too smart but you can be an asshole and it's a bonus point."

"You can't have pimples and you can't not have a boyfriend," Lily added.

"You can't not have boobs," I said.

"It's fucked up," said Bobby Castillo. His pretty lips sure could spew the four-letter words. I was impressed.

"We should start the anti-mean club," I said.

"Yeah. The mean people suck club."

The club for cool outcasts.

That was one club I wanted to belong to. I looked at Lily hunched in her sweatshirt, the sleeves pulled over her hands. She was cold, shivering slightly, even in the heat. Bobby Castillo, with his lean torso, his long, skinny legs, reclining on his side now, like a wildcat beside us. And me in roses. I realized that mean people had their purpose, too. They brought you together. They unified you. They made you find your friends.

MOUSETTE

That afternoon I decided to take myself out to the movies as Kurt had suggested. Though I wondered how much it was okay to go on imaginary dates with imaginary friends and when it got to be something you needed to see a doctor about.

But, a sign of looniness or not, I needed practice. I hadn't been to a movie since Charlie took me to *Funny Lady*, and I was working my way to asking Bobby and Lily out soon.

I rode the bus to Hollywood Boulevard and watched *Benji* at the Chinese Theater. I loved movies with dogs in them but Benji's sparky eyes and perky teeth made me want a dog so much that I kind of wished I had chosen to see something else, even *Funny Lady* again. To cheer myself up about not owning a dog, I went to Will Wright's and got a pistachio, chocolate, and strawberry ice-cream cone—my own Neapolitan mix. It was fun to be out by myself in Hollywood, tripping merrily along the stars with names famed and forgotten, thinking of my new friends and the pleasure I was having, even all alone. I bought a shirt that said HOLLYWOOD CALIFOR-NIA! and had some palm trees and shooting stars on it. I pretended I was a starlet on a date, waiting to be discovered. No one seemed to notice me at all but I didn't care—I was having fun!

Then I saw two people I recognized—Mimi Jones and Carla St. Clair from my building, so I followed them. They were hurrying along in their high heels, laughing and carrying shopping bags. They looked so happy and I wished I had a best friend like that. Then I was standing in front of the tall art-deco building that housed the Hollywood Museum—Carla and Mimi had gone inside. I looked up at the green marble facade and suddenly I understood.

Factor's fairest.

Max Factor.

The building had once been the place where famed Hollywood makeup artist Max Factor worked his magic on all the stars. Bette Davis, Jean Harlow, Rita Hayworth, Ginger Rogers, Judy Garland.

As I walked into the pink-and-white marble lobby decorated with potted palms and chandeliers, I wondered who had sent me here. And why?

There were individual little boudoir-style rooms for blondes, brunettes, brownettes, and redheads, filled with photos of actresses and painted to go with the appropriate hair colors (blue, mint green, rose, and peach, respectively). There were glass cases displaying the makeup the actresses used and wigs they had worn, like Billie Burke's blonde Glinda curls and Marlene Dietrich's twenty-karat gold-dusted wig. The blonde room was best, of course, because of Marilyn.

On the upper floor there were dresses she had worn in movies including a pink one from *Let's Make Love*, giant photos of her, including the famous *Playboy* nudes where her skin was like breathing marble, and even the last check she had signed. It made me want to cry to see her handwriting. It made her seem so real and so gone.

I had been here before, with Charlie and my mom, but I hadn't thought about it in years. Now everything in the building seemed to come alive. I could hear the whispers of the stars and smell their perfume. Satin and lamé swished and shimmered. Lights and gold dust twinkled in my brain.

I didn't know why I had been sent here but I felt better for having come. I felt hopeful like I'd just woken up from a beautiful dream I didn't quite understand.

I never found Mimi or Carla. I was starting to doubt I'd really seen them go into the museum at all.

As I was leaving I ran my fingers through my new haircut and asked the petite redhead at the desk what room I belonged in. She peered at me over her rhinestone-studded cat glasses, frowned crossly, and said, "We don't have a mousette room."

I couldn't help but laugh. Mousette. I didn't mind. It sounded unique. Besides, the redhead's hair was the color of burned tomato sauce and I had been called the fairest of them all. By someone, at least.

I headed for the door but Tomato called me back.

"Wait a second."

She sounded angry and I wondered if I had touched

something I shouldn't have or just offended her with my tasteless hair color.

I went back to her. "Yes?"

"I think I have something for you. What's your name?"

"Weetzie," I said.

"Weetzie. What kind of a name is that?"

I didn't really think it was any of her business but I said, "A diminutive of Louise. Like Brooks."

"She would never have hair that color," the woman said. "She was a true brunette!"

"What were you going to ask me?" I asked.

Grouchy handed me something from a drawer. It was a shiny envelope with my name written on it.

"For you."

"Who gave you that?"

"I'm not to tell. Now go on." She shooed me toward the door. "And don't come back until you're an actual shade of something."

Rude, but I didn't care. I jammed my finger under the flap and shimmied it open. There was another piece of paper and when I unfolded it, more glitter fell out. Luckily, I was on the sidewalk by this time so the red terror wouldn't yell at me.

The note read, in cutout letters:

Fee Fi Fo Fum
I smell the bones of an extinct one
Be she live or be she dead
I'll pay homage to her head

Now this one was kind of creepy. I felt a little sick to my stomach. Who was writing these? The man with the turban? The red-haired lady? Winter? That last one made me get a fluttering feeling in my rib cage. And how were the notes getting to me? And what did this one mean? It didn't make any sense at all.

But I wasn't going to let that ruin my mood. Whoever had written the first note had sent me to the Hollywood Museum and I was happy about that. Maybe the second note would take me somewhere special, too. I needed to think about it.

On the way to the bus I pretended I was a starlet on a date, waiting to be discovered, even with my mousette hair. This made me walk differently and my skin felt warm and shivery at the same time.

At home I put the note with the other one in my ballerina box and then went to swim some laps in the pool as the sun was setting. The water was still heated and all my muscles relaxed, flowing into blue light. Then I lay in a lounge chair, letting the breeze tingle my skin and watched the sky deepen from light blue to light pink to dark pink to purple, shades Max Factor would have admired on even the drabbest mousette.

At school the next day Lily found me.

"You look all glowy," she said as we walked to our new lunch spot.

"I took myself on a date."

She grinned. "They say in magazines you are supposed to do that to cheer yourself up."

"Exactly. It kind of worked. But I was practicing for when I get to hang out with you."

Bobby bounded up behind us.

"What's this about hanging out? I want to come."

Lily and I exchanged a secret smile. She was glowy now, too.

"Weetzie went on a date," she said.

"With who?"

"With myself!"

"Cool! But next time you better invite us."

So the next afternoon, Bobby and Lily and I took a bus to the Santa Monica Pier. The sky was grayish blue and the waves were steely teal. It was colder than normal and the air smelled starkly of salt. We walked along past the kids playing pinball, the vendors selling straw hats and beach toys, the fishermen brave or desperate enough to eat fish caught in the bay, and the stand-up cutouts of Marilyn and James Dean through which you could peek to have your picture taken. We played a game in the arcade and almost won a giant Pink Panther, but didn't.

"I think those games are cruel to plastic ducks, anyway," Lily said.

"And Pink Panthers are an endangered species," I added.

Bobby and I got ice-cream cones but Lily didn't want one and I didn't push—she looked as if I were going to stab her with my swirly pink-and-white confection when I held it out to offer her a taste. To take her mind off it, I suggested we ride the carousel. We waited in line with the little kids. The horses were painted glossy colors. They had carved saddles and wild eyes and flared nostrils. I remembered coming here with Charlie and how I made him stand beside me so I wouldn't fall off, the feel of his hands around my waist and the flash of his smoky grin. I realized that even though I missed him I was having fun without him and I didn't need anyone to hold me on anymore.

DREAM INVADERS
STARRING HYPATIA WIGGINS

I was feeling almost happy the next day when I skated home from school. I wasn't even thinking about my dad. The day was beautiful and brushed with gold. Palm trees rustled restlessly in the Santa Anas. Afternoons were almost as good as Saturdays. School was over and night had not come yet with its memories and ghosts and dreams.

But when I got home I found my mom crying on the couch.

"What's wrong?"

She pointed to the TV. On the screen a woman in a silver jumpsuit with her hair in a high ponytail, the kind only the very beautiful and very confident can pull off, was cavorting for the camera. It was my dad's sci-fi movie *Dream Invaders*, based on *A Midsummer Night's Dream,* and it had been a big flop. I hadn't seen it since I was a kid.

I stared at the woman. The movie was black and white but I recognized the shape, if not the color, of her eyes. Suddenly, I realized why the woman in number 13 looked familiar.

"Who is she?" I asked.

"Hypatia Wiggins," my mom hissed.

"What kind of name is that?"

My mom took a gulp of her drink and pointed at the TV. "No one just leaves," she said. "There is almost always someone else involved."

Then I remembered hearing the name—Hypatia Wiggins, how could you forget?—batted back and forth between my parents as they stood by the pool with the sky blooming toxic pink around them.

"What can I do for you?" I asked my mother.

"You can find out." She turned to me and her eyes were fierce. "Find out what happened. Why he left me."

• • •

So, that afternoon, instead of just relaxing and basking in the fact that I actually might have made a couple of friends, that I might be feeling all right even without Charlie, I went and knocked on the door of number 13 where the mysterious lady lived.

No one answered so I knocked again. I almost decided to leave—what did I think I was doing? But then I pushed really gently on the door and it opened.

I stood waiting for the dogs to come running but everything was quiet.

"Hello?" I said. "Anybody home?"

Silence.

I peeked inside. The condo had almost the same floor plan as ours, just smaller. It was dim and the brocade drapes were pulled closed. I whistled, waiting for the dogs to attack, but they didn't seem to be around. I slipped inside and locked the door behind me.

I wondered if I was making a mistake. Would this only make things worse? But maybe I'd be proven wrong. Or, at the very least, I might be able to find something to help my mom move on with her life.

The whole place smelled of incense like a fabric store in the Valley. Joy Grier used to take me and Skye and Karma there to buy fabric from bolts of cloth in bins collaged with magazine cutouts of naked ladies. The front room of the condo was sparsely furnished but the bar was stocked, even better than ours. There was a purple velvet sofa that my mom would have loved, a glass coffee table, and an entertainment center with a TV. Three matching brocade dog beds were on the floor. On the walls were framed modeling photographs of the woman wearing false eyelashes and elaborate hairdos and family photos of her with her arms around two children. The boy was fair and tall and the girl was thin and dark-haired. I recognized both of them.

None of them, in any picture, were smiling. Not in one single picture. I felt a chill along my shoulder blades.

I went to the first bedroom. On the door was a painted sign that said, *Annabelle's Room. Keep Out!* I didn't. The walls were painted an aggressive shade of pink and there was a fancy dressing table with a ruffled skirt and a large oval mirror. On the walls were pictures of movie stars from the 1950s. There was a huge collection of Barbie dolls scattered around the room. Most of them looked endangered, with blindfolds over their eyes, ropes around their wrists and ankles, tape over their mouths. Some had pins stuck into them or were missing limbs or even heads. Some had jewelry made out of what looked like tiny bird bones. I felt as if the dolls were watching me with their startled, always open, blue-shadowed eyes, asking me for help.

"Sorry," I told them, and ran out of the room. I was covered in a film of cold sweat as even as perfectly applied sunscreen.

In the room next door there were piles of skateboard magazines and unwashed clothes. A stereo stood in what appeared to be a place of honor and there were Doors, Beatles, Dylan, and Hendrix posters on the walls. The room smelled like dirty socks but there was something comforting about being there in contrast to the rest of the place and part of me wanted to stay, to snuggle into the unmade bed and sniff the sheets.

Instead, I went into the master bedroom. There was a waterbed with a red velvet bedspread. I jumped onto the bed and looked up at the mirrored ceiling. I saw myself floating on a bloodred ocean, thin and pale and seasick with dis-ease.

I flipped over on my stomach. There was a framed photo on the bedside table.

And I saw it.

It was a picture of Hypatia Wiggins wearing a red dress, her long dark hair piled on her head. She was leaning into the arms of a tall, thin man with a five o'clock shadow and dramatically high cheekbones.

I hadn't inherited those cheekbones but I knew them very well, sharp when I kissed them.

The man was my father. It was possible that he had been cheating on my mother with Hypatia Wiggins all this time.

That was when I heard the sound of keys in the lock and the dogs barking and scrambling at the door.

But this is what I knew: I knew the layout of the condo because it was just like mine. Here would be the main bathroom off the master bedroom. Here would be the small bathroom window. It was not painted shut. I stood on the toilet seat and opened it. My body was just small enough to slither through and jump onto a bench on the walkway before the three bears got home. Here would be safety, momentarily at least.

My father was gone and his photograph was on our new neighbor's bedside table. What did it mean? Had my dad been cheating on my mom? Is that why she drank so much, had changed so much? And what did that say about my relationship with Charlie? If he had been lying to my mom the whole time, what other lies did he tell us? I must be less important to him than he said I was if he could betray our family like that. If it was all true, he had also betrayed the woman he was cheating on us with, leaving her and running off to New York. I had been deluding myself the last couple of days. Charlie didn't have a crystal ball. He didn't care if I was good or bad, what I did or didn't do, how I dressed, if I left dirty dishes in the sink or even broke into strangers' homes. I didn't matter to my dad as much as I had thought. I didn't even really know who he was anymore.

That night I snooped through my dad's stuff looking for a picture of Ms. Wiggins or some sign of her. There were black notebooks filled with sketches and notes for the films my dad had worked on and boxes of dusty sci-fi screenplays. There was a collection of glass paperweights, including one of the Empire State Building. The snow inside had turned yellowish. I wondered if my dad was looking at the real Empire State Building right then.

I found an enamel pillbox with my dried-blood-spotted baby teeth and a lock of pale hair.

There was a black shoe box with a few black-and-white photographs of my dad and his sister, Goldy, with their parents in Brooklyn. In one he was standing in a bucket of water wearing a diaper and grinning. In another Goldy was holding him in her arms like he was a doll. Aunt Goldy had visited us in the cottage when I was born but my mom said she was judgmental and turned up her nose at the food my mom made so she was never invited back.

I saw more photos, too. There were some of me as a baby looking very bald and surprisingly fat with chub bracelets around my ankles and wrists. There was a wedding picture of my parents like dolls on a cake. It was shocking how young and beautiful and in love they looked. There was a photo of my dad's grandmother. Her children had to leave her behind when the Nazis came. She was too frail to travel and she made them go. Charlie always said that he hoped she'd died before she was taken but no one knew for sure. My great-grandma's eyes were hauntedly sad as if they knew what was coming.

I didn't want to see her eyes. What was I looking for? A copy of the picture I'd seen? Had I really seen it at all? Did missing my father so much and being so angry at him at the same time make me see it? Or was the affair with the purple-eyed woman real and my father had just covered his tracks, maybe taken any evidence of her away with him, tucked in his coat pocket, nearer to his heart than I might ever be again.

I put everything away and went to check on my mom who was sleeping in front of the TV in the same yellow negligee. It made me so sad to see her like that, in that shabby nightgown. I remembered the way she would only wear natural fabrics like silk or real cotton, the way she would paint her toenails like the tiny, shiny, pale-pink shell fragments we found on the beach. I remembered the dresses she made for me and the doll dresses she made from the scraps. Petal Bug still had one of them on.

I went into my room and found Petal Bug under the bed. The dress she wore had pink and purple flowers all over it. I could remember the skirt my mom made for me out of that fabric. It had burned in the fire.

Suddenly, I felt an overwhelming desire to make something pretty. But just as quickly I changed my mind. What was the point? The most beautiful thing of all—love—could change into two people screaming at each other and one of them driving away forever.

I climbed into bed and jammed Petal Bug under one arm and Mink under the other and thought about being in Winter's room without him knowing, being able to smell him when he wasn't there. I imagined him coming into my room in the dark and sitting at my bedside, stroking my forehead with his hand, whispering fairy tales the way my father used to, his blue eyes like night-lights.

After I'd fallen asleep I thought I heard the phone ring, a muffled sound, far away across the land of Nod. That's what my mom used to call it. By the time I reached it the caller had hung up.

THE BLOWS

The next day proved that I was right about not spending time on making something pretty to wear as a way to distract me from the realization that my dad had probably been cheating on my mom for years. When I got to school my scruffy jeans and sweatshirt didn't matter. No one was looking at my outfit but they were looking at me.

A low, ominous hum met me as I went up to the front gate. It was hundreds of voices whispering in unison at me.

"Blow blow blow blow blow."

On the walls of the building around the quad where we ate our lunch someone had scrawled graffiti—huge black letters, about twelve feet high.

The graffiti said:

BOBBY C. SUCKS DICK

LILY CHIN BLOWS CHUNKS

And last but not least (you guessed it):

LOUISE B. JUST BLOWS

I stepped backward and felt someone steady me with warm, delicate hands. It was Bobby.

"You okay?" he asked. The dark curls bounced merrily around his face but he wasn't smiling his usual mischievous grin.

"Are you?"

He nodded. "I'm thinking of mine as free advertising."

I socked him lightly in the shoulder. The janitors were already setting up their ladders to paint over the graffiti. But not before Lily had seen.

She was sitting by herself and we went over to her. She was crying.

Bobby threw himself down on the cement bench and put his head in her lap. She looked startled, then pleased, then confused. The tears kept streaming down behind her glasses and she dabbed them with her sweatshirt sleeve.

"Once they heard me. In the bathroom. And the next day they made this, this mess. It was all this disgusting cafeteria food mixed together." She shuddered. "They would leave globs of it around where I was. Once they put some on my notebook."

I had planned on telling Bobby and Lily about what had happened to me the day before, about the picture of my dad in Winter's apartment, but I decided I had to give all my attention to helping Lily then. I put my arm around her.

"I'd like to shove some of that stuff down Staci's throat," Bobby said.

I watched the janitors working on the graffiti. "How'd those girls get up there?" I said. "It would wreck their nails."

We looked across the yard at where Staci, Marci, and Kelli were holding court before three tall ninth-grade boys with broad biceps. Jeff Heller, Rick Rankin, and Staci's superhot stoner boyfriend, Casey Cassidy. They were all laughing hysterically. Oh.

"They won't mess with you again," I told Lily, although I had no idea how I was going to stop them. I wasn't thinking about impressing Charlie's nonexistent crystal ball or the fact that he wasn't who I'd thought he was—I just needed to find some way to help my friends.

I looked at Bobby. He pulled a square of Bubble Yum out of his Levi's pocket and handed it to me.

I had been practicing ever since the gum-in-hair incident, planning to someday challenge Staci Nettles to a duel. I unwrapped the gum. It had a thick, chalky texture and smelled of pink and sugar. I stuck it in my mouth and blew and blew—the biggest bubble I had ever made. It got bigger even than my face.

"I blow," I said.

After school I went to find Winter. I knew I had to talk to him about it all. I thought of being alone in his room, breathing his air. I thought of his eyes like blue mood-ring stones. Happiness. I thought of how he knew my father and now Charlie's picture was in his apartment. I thought about the mysterious notes I had received. Fee Fi Fo Fum.

My nerves had been jangled by that message. Now they were worse from the graffiti and seeing the picture of my dad. Something needed to start making sense.

I knocked on Winter's door and held my breath. What if the girl, Annabelle, or her mother, Hypatia, answered? If the mother did, I'd be face-to-face with the truth about my dad and I wasn't ready for that yet. What if the dogs answered? But there was no barking and all I saw when the door opened was Winter wearing khaki green army pants, which were a little too big so they hung low on his narrow hips, and a white T-shirt. The dogs growled behind him in the dim room. The incense smell hit me with its sensory memory of naked ladies on fabric bins.

"Hey," he said, smiling. When I saw that slow smile showing the white chewing-gum teeth I had to remind myself to be mad.

"You still mad?" he asked, reading my mind.

"I don't know who you are or why you are following me or how you know my dad," I said. "And why your crazy sister is attacking me and . . ."

I almost said something about the photo on his mother's bedside table but my heart banged a surge of blood to my head in warning and I stopped.

"How do you know she's my sister?" He squinted at me from under the lock of hair. I couldn't tell what he was thinking. He could have been suspicious or just curious. I could have been paranoid from all my snooping.

"Isn't she?"

"Pretty much." He reached behind his back for his skateboard and stepped outside. "Want to go somewhere? I got to get out of here."

I nodded a little reluctantly, trying to see into the condo before he closed the door (was there really that photograph of my father on his mother's bedside table?), and followed him like a helpless puppy down the stairs and out the front gate.

I put my skates back on and then he zipped off, so I went after him. (Remember: he was the cutest boy who had ever paid any attention to me in my entire life.) We went east a ways, then north toward the hills, sloping gray under the afternoon haze. The apartment buildings and houses were older there, many in Spanish styles with red-tiled roofs and thick adobe walls. We turned onto a small side street. There was a little deserted park with a swing set and climbing equipment. The patch of sand and green was surrounded by a wall of bamboo overgrown with morning glories, bougainvillea, and oleander, all intertwined to create a new plant of purple bells, red leafy blossoms, and hot-pink-and-white flowers. A white angel's trumpet with its poisonous, upside-down lily cups grew nearby. Winter jumped onto one of the swings and gestured for me to join him. His long legs looked like they could touch the sky.

I scowled at him for a while but it didn't seem to be working so I went over and sat on the swing, dragging my skates in circles in the sand.

"It's better if you actually swing," Winter said, smiling at me sideways. "That's why they call it a swing?"

"I don't feel like it."

He slowed down and twisted the chain swing so that he was facing me.

"Are you sending me those notes?" I asked.

"What notes?" He blinked innocently, fluttering his eyelashes the way an actor would do in a movie, but it felt genuine.

"Fairest of them all? Fee Fi Fo Fum?"

"Nursery rhymes?"

"Yes. Did you send them?"

He shook his head. "It's been a long time since I heard any nursery rhymes. Why?"

I decided to let that one go. I had a more important question. "How do you know Charlie?"

"He was my mom's director. I guess they were friends."

"Friends? Yeah right."

"Believe me, Weetzie, whatever the situation is, you're the one he cares about the most."

"Cares? He left me! He hasn't even called."

"He thinks about you all the time."

"How do you know?" I got up and moved away from

him. My heart was doing its slamming thing. I saw red. You know how they say you see red when you're angry? That was really what it was like. The world looked red for a second like when you press your hands over your eyelids and tilt your face up toward the sun.

Winter looked down at his hands and bit nervously at one cuticle. "He's tried to call you," he said. "But she always answers. Or the machine."

I slumped on the bench and put my head down. "Why is this happening?"

Winter untwisted the chain of his swing and spun away from me, rubbing his eyes with a fist. "My dad left, too," he said.

When he stopped spinning I saw that his eyes were red. "I never really got to know him at all. He was always doing his own thing and working so hard. All I got from him is this fucked-up last name."

"I'm sorry." It was the first time I had stopped thinking about myself that afternoon.

"But then I realized that the whole thing is bullshit—this parent-child thing. Some people are lucky to have it but a lot of them don't. You just have to make your own family, your own life. Whatever. Even when you're a kid and it feels too hard. That's the only way. You have to figure out how to take care of yourself before anything else will work out."

I nodded and watched him squinting into the tangle of foliage around us.

"This is beautiful," he said. "Here. That's another thing you've got to do. You've got to see the beauty whenever you can and take what you can get. Otherwise you just get old."

"Like Charlie," I said. "He got old. And my mom, too."

Winter tossed his hair out of his eyes and leaned back in the swing, stretching his arms up behind him and cracking his knuckles. "They all do. But not me. I'll never get old." There wasn't teenage invincible, live-forever bravado in his voice—he sounded a little melancholy, almost.

The day seemed to get darker and cooler all at once. A blackbird cawed ominously in a tree overhead and I wanted to leave. I had seen the beauty in things before, when I was a kid, but I wasn't so sure about it anymore. Even the prettiest flowers were toxic. I wondered if thinking like that would make me old at thirteen.

Winter stood up and reached for my hand. My skates were unsteady in the sand.

"He'll call," Winter said. "Just make sure you answer the phone."

We got back to our building and he looked at me

for a moment before we said good-bye. The sadness on his face was back, like the real Winter revealed under a warrior's metal mask. I wanted to hug him but I didn't. It would have been impossible for me to let go.

"Get that phone, Weetzie Bat," he said.

When it rang that night while we were watching TV, I pounced on it. My mom was dozing in her chair and didn't notice.

"Daddy?" I almost screamed it before he had even said hello. There was a long silence. Then the sound of a man clearing his throat.

"Hi, baby."

My mom stirred in the chair and moved her hands around as if she were swatting at an imaginary fly. "Who is it?" she slurred, but her eyes were half closed.

"Just a friend from school." I whispered into the phone, "I'm going to pick it up in my room. Don't hang up. Don't hang up, okay?"

He made a soft sound.

"Okay?"

"Okay, Weetz."

I placed the phone down and ran into my room. He was still there.

"What are you doing?" I saw that my hands were

shaking with adrenaline but they didn't even feel like mine. "Why did you leave without telling me? Where are you? You didn't call!"

"I tried," he said softly. His voice was hoarse. "I'm sorry, Weetzie."

It was the sound of him saying my name that broke me into little pieces. Tears burned in my sinuses.

"Sweetie?" He waited while I took a breath, rough as if my throat were corrugated. "Are you okay?"

"No," I said. "I miss you. I want to go with you."

"I'm sorry, sweetheart. You can't go with me."

"Where are you?"

"I'm in New York. You need to stay and take care of your mother."

I picked up the Empire State Building paperweight he had left behind. I had known he was there all along. Where else would he be? I squinted my eyes and saw a tiny Charlie and a tiny Weetzie waltzing inside of the glass ball. She was gazing up at him like he was a shining monument.

"Take care of her?" I said. "She's supposed to take care of me. So are you."

"I will, honey. I'll send money. I have to straighten some things out."

"Like what?" I wanted to scream at him but I kept

my voice soft so my mother wouldn't hear. "Like how to bring your new girlfriend and her kids with you? Your buddy Winter and his crazy sister? Is that it?"

"Weetzie? What are you talking about?"

"Do you think I'm stupid? I'm not a little kid. I know what it looks like."

"What things look like is not necessarily what they are." He sounded so sad. I imagined him resting his head in his hand, stroking his stubbled chin with his palm. He cleared his throat. "Weetzie, I'm not with anyone right now, all right? I had to get away from everything and get my head straight."

I heard a click and my mom's voice. "Hello? Are you still on the phone, Louise? Who is it?"

And then, with that, Charlie was gone.

The first thing I wanted to do was run over to number 13 and knock on the door, wake that woman, shake her, and scream at her for ruining my life. But what I really wanted was for her son to answer and hold me in his arms and give me the comfort my father no longer could.

Instead, I lay in bed and thought about being in the yellow VW Bug with Winter. We would have the stereo on and the sun was shining in and sometimes as we drove through the tangled, green canyons and along the shore pulsing with blue ocean light he would look over, smile, and put his hand on my thigh in its jeans.

"I'll take care of you," he would say.

That didn't happen. The touching part or the thing he said. But Winter did take me for a drive in his VW one day.

It was Saturday and there was a knock on the door. I answered without thinking. I was wearing cutoffs and my pajama shirt and my hair was a nest for rats.

Winter was standing with his skateboard tipped up by one foot. He shook his hair out of his eyes but it fell back immediately.

"Hey."

"Hey," I gulped. I could feel my face turning the color of my pink flannel pajama shirt.

"What's up?"

"Uh. Not much. Just waking up." I looked down at my outfit.

"Sorry. I was just wondering if you wanted to go for a drive or something. Where we could talk." He peered behind me, toward the living room, and I knew he was thinking about my mom, wanting to avoid her.

"Uh. Sure. Yeah. Hang on."

"I'll meet you downstairs," he said, grabbed his

skateboard, and disappeared so fast that it made me wonder if I had imagined the whole thing.

I washed and dressed quickly, to the rhythm of my pounding heart, praying it was real and that if it were he wouldn't leave. Shower. Secret. Jeans. T-shirt. Lip gloss. Bye, Mom. Gone.

He was waiting for me, leaning against the Bug like a boy in a movie. At that moment it was as if nothing sad had ever happened to me. It is so strange the way the chemicals in our brain can work like that—erasing all the sorrow with one rush of joy, even if it isn't really real.

We drove east, not talking, just listening to the cassette he played, a woman's raspy voice singing over raucous chords. She was whispering something about horses again and again. I'd never heard anything like it.

Finally, I asked who she was.

"Patti Smith. Isn't she cool?" He handed me the cassette. It had a picture of a gaunt, androgynous person in a white shirt, a string of black tie hanging loose around her neck. I wondered if I should try wearing one of Charlie's ties.

"Your dad likes her," he said.

My dad? A little drumbeat of jealousy shook me from inside. Why was my dad talking about music with this boy? He had never even mentioned Patti Smith to me. I scratched at the denim encasing my thigh. How stupid was I for getting excited about going out with Winter? He'd never be interested in me. This was all arranged by my father.

Winter turned north up Beachwood. The houses spilled down the hillsides with their gardens of avocados, plum and lemon trees that you could live off of if you had to, their high walls and windows overlooking the city beneath the Hollywood sign.

The sign used to read Hollywoodland my dad had told me. Hollywoodland. Holly Woodlawn, the famous transsexual who was part of Andy Warhol's Factory. Holly Golightly, Truman Capote's character from *Breakfast at Tiffany's*, played by Audrey Hepburn in the movie, standing in the rain kissing George Peppard and squishing Cat between their wet trench coats. Holly and Ivy, plants and names of two of my dolls who had burned in the cottage fire. Hollyberries for which the land was named. I let the words run through my head so I wouldn't have to think about what was happening. Why was Winter taking me out with him on a Saturday? If this beautiful boy wasn't interested in me, what did he plan to do? In a beat, the music sounded ominous, even sinister. I imagined the headline: Teen Girl's Body

Found at Base of Hollywood Sign: Skateboard Killer At Large. I thought about Peggy Entwistle, the blonde actress who had jumped to her death from the sign in 1932. She had died of multiple fractures to her pelvis. I wondered how long it took her to die and if the coyotes got to her. The day she'd died she had received a letter informing her that she had gotten the lead part in a play, playing a woman who kills herself in the first act. I wondered if the news would have made her reconsider.

We wound higher and stopped where the road ended at a fire road gate. Winter got out. I followed him like a puppet with a wooden stick for a spine and strings attached to my arms and legs. I realized that I didn't care that much what happened to me. I suddenly just felt really tired.

He sat on the hillside under the sign and I sat, too. The grasses were parched, yellow, and scratchy around us and the city spread out below under that blue-gray layer of haze. Winter didn't look like a murderer. He didn't even have his skateboard to hit me over the head with. We stared out at the city. My dad always said that the best parts of L.A. were the high places, like the Hollywood sign and the Griffith Observatory and Mulholland Drive, where you could look down at it and pretend the city was just a pretty expanse of lights and not a cultural wasteland full of broken dreams.

"Did you hear from him?" Winter asked as if he had read my mind again. It wasn't hard to figure out what I was thinking about, but still. I wondered if Winter had brought me all the way there just to ask me that.

I nodded. That was all I was going to give him.

"That's good. Right?" He looked over at me.

"Why are you doing this?" I turned on him. The woman's voice was still in my head. *Horses horses horses.*

"Doing what?"

"Why do you care about what happens with me and my dad?"

He was quiet for a little while. Then he said, "I'm trying to help."

I stood and stamped my feet like a kid having a tantrum. "But why? Why do you care? Why should I even trust you at all?"

"Weetzie!" He leaped up beside me. It was the first time I'd seen him angry since he'd called the dogs off. But now he was angry at me. "I don't know why I tried to help you!" He kicked at some dirt with the toe of his shoe. "Let's get out of here."

He was heading back down the hill.

"Wait!" I said. "I'm sorry." I wanted to explain to him about all the things that had built up inside me.

The loss of my trust in Charlie and my jealousy of Purple Woman and my crush on Winter that would never come to anything and how I wanted him to kiss me and how I had imagined he was going to kill me and throw my body off the top of the Hollywood sign. I couldn't say any of it. He already thought I was crazy.

He turned back to me. His voice was a little softer now but his eyes didn't focus on mine. "Listen. It was a bad idea, okay? I don't know why I brought you here. I need to get back now."

I followed him the rest of the way, down into what my dad called the boneyard of broken dreams.

My dad didn't call again. My mother drank. I understood this more now, why she'd been drinking ever since around the time of that photograph in Winter's apartment. I understood it but I still didn't know what to do about it really, except to try to make food for her and hide the bottles whenever I could. I tried to accept my new haircut, even though it made me feel dorky and naked and seemed to overemphasize the exaggerated uptilt of my nose and the saucer shape of my eyes. I tried to concentrate in class but my grades were slipping. My skin broke out a little around my chin. I ignored Staci, Marci, and Kelli when they swept by me

99

with their slack-jawed, evil-eyed boyfriends. I ignored it when Jeff Heller came up behind me in the hall and goosed me through my jeans, his fingers grabbing me so hard that I almost vomited. I ignored it when Casey Cassidy barked at me and Lily, although I wanted to flip him off. I ignored it when Rick Rankin passed me and my friends and growled, "The fag, the dog, and the freak," even though Bobby flipped him off and Lily looked like she was going to cry. I tried not to think about Winter's sister or his perilously beautiful mother who had lured my father away from Brandy-Lynn or about the fact that now he had left us all.

Days just happened to me, and then nights.

I didn't hear from Winter and I didn't go looking for him but I thought about him every night before I fell asleep and sometimes I dreamed that he was sitting at my bedside telling me fairy tales like my dad used to. It felt so real that when I woke up I was startled Winter wasn't there.

I was lonely but not as much as the Lonely Doll was before she met the bears. I invited Lily and Bobby over to my place. My mom hardly noticed. Every afternoon we went into my room and sloshed around on my water-bed and crunched around on my beanbag chairs and ran our fingers through the plastic bead curtains that hung around my bed. We listened to Led Zeppelin and tripped out on the album cover art of the naked blonde kids scrambling over the psychedelic rocks. One day Bobby brought a joint. The smoke hurt my lungs and I didn't get what the big deal was but afterward we made Pillsbury chocolate chip cookies and ate the whole batch (well, Bobby and I did). I have to admit chocolate had never tasted so good. Then we went swimming in the pool in the light rain that had started to fall. When I saw Lily in her baggy one-piece navy-blue bathing suit I got scared because you could see almost every bone in her body like a plastic Halloween skeleton but I didn't want to think about it too much. I didn't want to hurt her feelings either. Some people were just skinny, right?

After we went swimming she was shivering and her face looked bluish so I wrapped her in a towel and we went back upstairs.

Lily took a shower and I gave her a terry cloth sweat suit to wear and then we all lay on my bed and cuddled and I made them listen to Janis Ian singing "At Seventeen." Lily and I had tears sliding down our cheeks while Bobby made fun of the song—ugly girls bemoaning the lack of love that beauty queens owned—but he did so only halfheartedly.

Finally, he said, "'At Seventeen'? How about at

fucking thirteen? Man."

"Not enough syllables," I said. "But otherwise it's perfect."

Lily nestled closer into my arms. She felt like a bony ten-year-old.

"I like being part of this club," she said.

Bobby laughed and blew a sugary pink bubble with his gum. "The Blowhards," he said.

When we got to school the next day it looked as if Staci Nettles had been initiated into our club, too.

On the wall where our names had been was written:

STACI N. IS A HORE

Sic. Casey or Jeff or Rick or all three of them couldn't even spell it right.

When I saw Staci in class it looked like she'd applied too much blusher and she had a startled, blank look in her eyes. The expression seemed wrong on her, unfamiliar, like if she'd suddenly dyed her hair a different color. I wanted to do something—laugh in her face or tell her I was sorry or remind her that being mean sucked but it didn't seem like any of the options were right so I just sat quietly and avoided looking at her while everyone else snickered, just as they had at me after my fifteen minutes of graffiti fame.

But when I ran into her in the hall I couldn't help asking if she was okay.

"What do you think?" she snarled.

I wasn't sure what she meant by that. Did she mean, *Of course I'm okay. I'm always okay*, or *Would you be okay if someone called you a hore (sic) in twelve-foot letters?*

Even pretty, popular girls got brutalized in junior high. I thought they were immune.

Blow.

Dick.

Blow.

Chunks.

Blow.

Job.

Blow.

Hore.

Sic.

Sick.

Suck.

It sucked being us.

WHO-DO VOODOO? YOU-DO VOODOO

*W*hen I got home from school that day (Lily and Bobby were home sick with colds from our swim in the rain, still innocent to the news about the new graffiti), Staci Nettles was there. For a second I thought she had come to see me. Had she realized the error of her evil ways after what she had been through?

I jumped behind a post and watched her. There were a few stray flecks of mascara on her smooth, tan cheeks but otherwise she looked as perfect as ever.

I was still standing there, staring at her shiny, watermelon lip-glossed mouth like a geek, wondering why she had come, when she passed by me and went up the stairs.

To Winter's.

Was she seeing Winter? Was she seeing his crazy sister? His mother? I wanted to barge in behind her and confront all of them, ask Purple Eyes what she was up to with my dad but instead I ducked behind the staircase and heard Staci knock on the door. The dogs barked. The door opened. Winter answered. I could hear him telling the dogs to be quiet.

"Hey," Staci said in her lushest lip-glossy voice.

There was a pause. Then Winter said, "Yes?"

"How's it going?" Staci asked.

"Can I help you?" Winter sounded cold and I felt relief inflate my narrowed chest.

"Is your sister here?"

That was all I heard. The door closed and with the sound, my chest deflated again.

I ran around to the back stairs and found the bathroom window from which I had escaped before. It was open. I climbed up on a crate and tried to listen but I couldn't hear. So I went around to the front.

It was time to visit Winter.

I knocked. The dogs barked again and I tensed, remembering the way they had looked when they were about to attack. At this point what lay inside those walls was more dangerous than having three vicious dogs sicced on me. There was the danger of my useless crush on Winter. There was the danger of Staci Nettles, who, for some reason, was visiting him and might come between us in some way. There was the danger of the girl with the laugh. There was the danger of seeing Brandy-Lynn's rival in her purple pantsuit and being reminded of the fact that she and Charlie had been together once and the choking feeling of not being able to tell her what I thought about that. And there was the danger of realizing that my entire past up until that point was nothing like I thought it had been. There was the danger of having all the good memories of my father (all that I had left of him at the moment) destroyed.

I knocked again.

Winter answered, commanding the dogs to be quiet.

"Weetzie?"

I wondered why it was a question.

"Can I come in?" I asked softly.

"Sure. What's up?"

I walked into the room with the purple couch

and tried not to stare at the photographs, looking for another one of my father. The dogs whined at me from their fancy beds. I wondered if they really could smell all the fear on me like perfume or sweat.

"We can go into my room," he said. "It's a mess, though."

He pushed some clothes aside off the bed and gestured for me to sit. Then collapsed into a pile of limbs on the floor and looked up at me. I was having trouble breathing. It was weird to be here for the reason I was, trying to figure out why Staci had come, but it was also weird to think that I'd been here before, without his knowing. The smell of him on the sheets felt too intimate and I almost got up and left.

"You okay?"

I wanted to say, "What do you think?" but I didn't.

"Um, can I have some water or something?"

"Sure." He left the room. I leaned my head against the wall and heard voices through the thin plaster.

Staci was saying, "Will it work?"

The other voice replied, "Did it work before?"

"But that was a love thing."

"It'll work."

"Because I want him to suffer."

There was a long silence, some rustling. Then the

other voice said in a low growl that seethed and buck-led with hatred, even through the walls: "I know."

I shivered with a sudden blast of cold as if someone had put on the air-conditioning, thinking of the Barbie dolls in their ropes and blindfolds, their necklaces of bones. Fee Fi Fo Fum.

Winter came back into the room with a glass of water and a bag of Cheetos.

I stood up. "I got to go," I said. "You guys have com-pany."

"No. Annabelle has company."

"Oh?" I tried to sound as innocent as possible. "I thought I recognized the voice?"

"You know her. Staci something. That girl from your school. They do some kind of weird girly shit in there. Don't ask me."

"The one who put gum in my hair you mean. The pretty one."

He shrugged. "I guess so."

It felt as if he'd slapped me. But at the same time I knew that reaction was wrong. What did I want from him? To deny she was pretty. To say he was sorry he let her in because she'd been mean to me. I was still act-ing like he owed me something, even though he'd been the one helping me. But I couldn't stop the feelings taunting me like Staci herself whispering in my ear.

"I don't think Staci Nettles would appreciate it if she knew I was here," I said.

"You can't worry too much about what people like that think."

I knew he was trying to be nice but I got up anyway.

"Weetzie?" His eyes were soft as the velvet of his mother's couch and his tone had a hint of something I wanted to believe was melancholy—or should I say, melancholy that had something to do with me. I wanted to stay with him but I knew I couldn't. I was just a charity case. Maybe he wasn't falling for Staci Nettles but that didn't mean he was interested in me, or that he'd ever think of me as more than a sad little girl. I should never have knocked on his door. Now not only was I reminded that Winter would never like me the way I wanted him to, would never *like* like me, but I also knew that Staci and Annabelle were trying to make another person suffer, not to mention the fact that I was in the home of my mother's rival, who I still didn't have the guts to confront. Great.

"See ya, Winter," I said as casually as I could, as if I were tossing off a cap that I really wanted to smash down on my head and never remove.

Casey Cassidy wasn't at school the next day or the

next. I wouldn't have thought twice about it except that when he did show up, his previously perfect, tan skin was covered with oozing red welts. He was wearing a cotton hat pulled down low over his eyes and he had some kind of beigey-pink lotion dabbed on the spots. Clearasil, I thought. I'd used it but I'd never seen anyone who needed it so badly, or so suddenly. He even had a couple of small round Band-Aids stuck on.

"Gross" was the word humming through the hallways.

"Gross" and "What happened?"

I remembered him barking at Lily and me but when he passed us that day he kept his eyes lowered.

What the hell was going on?

I was bothered by it all day and I asked Lily and Bobby what they thought.

"Bad skin day," Bobby said. "Poor baby."

"It happened overnight." I felt something stirring in my mind but I hadn't quite gotten there yet. "Staci was at my neighbor's house," I told them.

They didn't know about Winter and his sister yet. It had all seemed too weird and would involve me getting into my dad leaving, which I didn't want to do.

"Your neighbor?" Lily asked. "You have some popularity princess living in your building?"

"No, just this disturbed girl. She's really creepy. Staci was over there and I sort of overheard them talking."

Bobby and Lily just stared at me. I fidgeted.

"Well?" Bobby finally said. "The suspense is killing me, Miss Blow."

"Something about wanting someone to suffer. Some guy."

"No shit!" Bobby's eyes looked more catlike than ever. I expected him to start purring with delight in a minute.

"So you think this weird neighbor girl and Staci made Casey's skin break out?" Lily didn't look as amused.

"I have no idea," I said. "I just know that it's weird. Plus, this girl, she has Barbies in her room with blindfolds and pins in them and stuff."

"Who do voodoo? Do you do voodoo?" Bobby was doubled over laughing but Lily still wasn't buying it.

"You give that girl way too much power, Weetz," she said.

"Not Staci. The girl. Anna. Or Annabelle. Whatever. She's really psycho. One time she sicced her dogs on me."

Bobby stopped laughing and they both stared at me again.

"Why didn't you tell us?" he asked.

"It happened before we started hanging out. She's been leaving me alone now."

"But why would she want to hurt you in the first place?" Lily hugged her knees to her chest and shivered.

"I told you. She's crazy." I didn't want to get into the whole thing with Winter and my dad's photo. I still didn't understand it all anyway. I was pretty sure Charlie and Winter's mom had been having an affair and that she decided to move too close and he had taken off. He and my mom were having problems anyway. He just couldn't deal with any of it. He wasn't the person I thought he was. But I didn't really know why he had left. I just knew that he was gone and the whole world looked different now.

"Well, she may be crazy but I sure wouldn't want her pissed at me," Bobby said.

"I'm scared," said Lily. Bobby leaned over and kissed her cheek. She turned pink as a sunset made from smog. I went around to the other side of her and we huddled together as if we could keep away the forces of evil if we stayed close enough, at least until the bell rang.

There was more that came out of Staci's mysterious visit to Winter's psycho sister than just Casey Cassidy's dermatological problems, let me tell you.

The next day after school, when I walked outside, I recognized the VW Bug before I saw him. He parked in a loading zone and got out slowly, not with the usual bounding step. He closed the door and stood in the street for a second.

A car honked at him and he startled, then shuffled up the curb and toward me.

I almost said his name out loud. I almost ran to him and asked him what was wrong.

But he hadn't come for me.

"Hey, Wiggins."

I turned around. Staci was shiny in the sunlight, wearing tight jeans that zipped around her crotch from the front to the back, the highest platform Kork-Ease, and a shirt she had unbuttoned and tied up just below her boobs as soon as the bell rang. Her abs were tan and toned and her waist was so small Winter could have cinched it with his hands like the stretchy rainbow cinch belts that she sometimes wore.

Marci and Kelli were standing back a little ways. I'd noticed they seemed to be less attentive to her since the graffiti incident. I grabbed Lily's arm.

"What's wrong?" she asked me.

Bobby was narrowing his eyes at everybody, trying

to sleuth out what was happening.

"Hi, Staci." Even Winter's voice sounded different—heavy and thick.

She flounced over to him and stood, shifting her hips and tossing her hair. "Got a ride for me?"

She grabbed his hand, waved at her friends, and dragged him to the Bug. Then Winter and Staci got in and drove away. She stuck her hand out of the window and waved. I realized that the armpits of my nice T-shirt were damp with sweat. Had I forgotten my Secret or was I just more upset than usual? I tried to remember my morning routine. Had I reached for the roll-on or not? It suddenly seemed terribly urgent.

"Weetzie?" Bobby said, somewhere from another planet.

"You okay?" I heard Lily but she was far away, too.

"I know him," I said. "Or I guess I thought I did." Then I turned to my friends. "Can we go to someone else's house today?"

We went to Bobby's house because Lily's mom was a screamer according to Lily and would force-feed us meat loaf. Bobby lived with his mom and half sister in a one-bedroom apartment. He slept on the convertible couch under a dangerous-looking swag lamp. No one

was home so we watched TV and ate popcorn on Bobby's bed. The Hallmark greeting-card commercials and
the phone company commercials and even the Coke
commercials made me cry.

It shouldn't have mattered that much. Winter and
Staci, I mean. But it did. Winter had become the substi-
tute for my dad since the day that beautiful boy pulled
my mother from the pool. One phone call, a few photos,
a few shirts and scripts, and a box of my own baby teeth
was about all I had left of Charlie. Even though I had
hardly spent any time with Winter and even though I
spent almost all of my time with Bobby and Lily now,
Winter was still who I secretly relied on in my imagina-
tion, who I thought of every night before I went to bed
to help me both feel connected to my dad and forget
that he was gone. I'd linked Winter and my father in
my mind and so it mattered much more than it would
have otherwise that a boy I hardly knew was acting like
a freak and going out with another girl. It mattered way,
way too much. I needed to stop thinking about both
Winter and my dad. Solving mysteries might be one
way to forget.

At home that evening I went to my ballerina music box
and took out the note from the Hollywood Museum.

I had put it out of my mind but now, while the music tink-tinkled and the ballerina turned on one toe, I read the note over and over again. Fee Fi Fo Fum. Giants. And something about bones. The bones of an extinct one. I remembered the tiny bone jewelry Annabelle had made for her poor, trapped Barbies. Was there some connection between Annabelle and the notes? Or was that just another weird coincidence in my weird life? No matter what, I wanted to find out what the notes meant. The last note had taken me somewhere I needed to go, somewhere that made me feel better, and maybe this one would do the same. I sure needed it. It seemed unlikely that Annabelle would have been involved in sending me to the Hollywood Museum just so I would hear that I was a mousette and cry about Marilyn's last check. There were too many good things there—like that dress from *Let's Make Love* with its halter top and flowing skirt dyed in gradations of pink, from blush to rose to hot, and wigs made of gold dust—for it to have been her. But if not Annabelle, then who? And where was I supposed to go next?

Extinct one.

Who was extinct? The little Weetzie who had believed that everyone would be okay, that her family would live happily ever after, that no monsters named fire or fear or anger or leaving would come.

Through my window I smelled a whiff of tar from the freshly applied blacktop.

With that inhale, I remembered something from a time, before.

Little Weetzie running barefoot down a grassy bank toward some water. Her father is following her. He doesn't want her to go there but she isn't listening to him, just giggling, running down the hill through the sunshine above and squishy mud below. But the water is black! She stops. It smells funny. Her dad picks her up and puts her on his shoulders. He carries her across the park to the big black pit of tar behind the chain-link fence. He is trying to distract her, make her smile at the statues of the elephants in the murky, bubbling pond. But she starts to cry when she sees them. Because while the daddy and the baby elephant stand on the bank, the mother is drowning in tar.

They're not elephants, he tells her. They're mastodons, they're extinct. But that doesn't cheer her up at all. In fact, it makes things worse.

Once, in prehistoric times, Los Angeles had just been this big pit of black tar and then it became a city and they built a museum on top of the tar pits. That's where

I went the next day after school, when I figured out what the note meant. I didn't invite Bobby and Lily because it seemed important for me to have another date with myself after everything that had happened.

I went into the actual museum first, and saw the gold-framed paintings of ladies reclining in rose gardens, the portraits of stiff-looking royalty in ermine, velvet, and jewels, the statues of fauns chasing nymphs, the ancient gold necklaces glimmering in glass boxes.

"This is not a museum," my dad used to say. "Where are the van Goghs? Where are the twenty-foot Buddhas? Someday I'll take you to the Met."

It wasn't New York, but still, it was culture (culture *with* statues of extinct animals popping out at you along the paths surrounding the museum).

I crossed the broad expanse of lawn and stood at the fence watching the mastodons. The family was in exactly the same position as always, the baby and the daddy watching the mama sink into black ooze, forever and ever.

I felt a little like the now-extinct baby statue when my father left. It was my father and not my mother who left, but my mother was sinking, too.

Why had I been sent here? To be reminded of this? I thought of Annabelle again, but, of course, she didn't know about my experience with the tar pits. Only my parents knew and Charlie couldn't have written the notes—he was too far away, and my mom was too drunk all the time.

I went back toward the museum and sat in the courtyard where we used to come to watch the mimes on weekends. My dad imitated them behind their backs and once one almost got into a fistfight with him. I don't even think it was a pretend mime-style fistfight but we didn't have time to find out because my mother and a lady mime, who was imitating her without her knowing it, intervened.

I hadn't seen a mime in quite some time so I was surprised when I turned and noticed what appeared to be a statue of one standing behind me. Of course, if you know anything about pesky mimes, you'll know it wasn't a statue but a mime doing one of their mimey games. This one had on red-and-white-striped tights, black knickers, a long-sleeved black shirt, and a black top hat. His face was painted white with red circles on his cheeks and lots of black makeup around his eyes. He had that eerie mime-ishness and I just stared at him, waiting for him to stop being a statue. Finally, I got tired of waiting and so I got up to leave. But somehow as I crossed the courtyard he was there, on the other side as if he'd just appeared—poof! It was freaky. I frowned at him and he bowed and tipped his hat, offered me an imaginary rose to sniff. I pretended it was stinky. He seemed to like that because he doubled over in hysterical, silent mime laughter. His teeth looked very yellow against his white face. After a few more convulsions he sobered up, reached into his pocket, and pulled out a silver envelope.

Just like the other two I'd received.

"Where'd you get that?" I yelped. But, of course, mimes aren't the best people to ask about this type of thing. Or anything, actually. "Please tell me!"

He handed me the letter, bowed, and scamperpranced off. I considered running after him but the idea of chasing a mime all through the tarry park just sounded too ridiculous to handle right then. Besides, I had a letter to open.

I opened it.

The note was just like the others. There was silver glitter inside and the letters were cut out from magazines. They spelled this:

Welcome Beauty, banish fear
My movie queen and mistress here
Kiss your wishes, speak your will
Swift obedience meets them still.

It was just as mysterious as the other ones had been. I would have to study it and figure out what it meant. But for now I had other things to think about—even the mime with the message hadn't been enough to distract me from my worries about my dad. And Winter.

HALLOWEETZIE

*I*t was Halloween. I was home with Bobby and Lily, painting black marks on their white-powdered faces to make them look like skulls. Bobby wore a top hat and a black suit with a white shirt, a black bolo tie, and cowboy boots. Lily wore a high-collared white-lace dress. I still hadn't decided what to put on. My hair was in tiny pigtails and I had on my polyester gym sweats with holes in them and one of my dad's ratty T-shirts. My friends and I had thought we were going to go trick-or-treating but it seemed childish and we were afraid no one would give us candy because we were way too big. We wanted to go see *The Exorcist* but it wasn't playing anywhere and it was rated R anyway. So we were home stuffing our faces with the 3 Musketeers bars Bobby had brought over for trick-or-treaters and wondering what we were going to do later.

The doorbell rang and we went to the door together. My mom had locked herself in her bedroom to avoid the noise. For a second I checked my reflection in the oval mirror with the gilt frame. I looked bad but so what? It was just little kids out there, kids in masks that obscured their vision. Plus, they only had eyes for the candy anyway, right?

But it wasn't little kids.

Two people stood at my door.

Staci Nettles was dressed as Cleopatra in a black wig, a gold bikini top, and a long, gold skirt. She had a gold snake bracelet winding up her arm and gold sandals on her feet.

She had a chain and it was attached to the neck of a male slave dressed only in harem pants and flip-flops.

I dug my nails into Bobby's arm and he flinched but didn't pull away.

It was Winter. His eyes were blank discs like he'd

been drugged. He was mumbling to himself and wouldn't look at me. My heart felt like a smashed and rotting pumpkin.

"Trick or treat," Staci said brightly. She batted her fake gold eyelashes at me and held out a pillowcase full of candy.

"Aren't you too old for this?" Bobby said. My hands were shaking like the fronds on the palm trees outside but I forced myself to give out the chocolates. Staci smiled and led Winter away. Behind them, then, I saw a third person. She was dressed in a low-cut pink satin gown. There was a long chiffon scarf around her neck and it looked like it had been dipped in blood. She had a black pillowcase over her head and in her hand was a mannequin's head in a blonde wig, also painted with blood.

"Who are you supposed to be?" Bobby couldn't help it—she just looked too weird.

The girl only held out her bag, and Lily put some candy in.

"Are you with them?" Bobby asked her but she had already left.

He turned to Lily. "Why'd you give her anything? She's another of Staci's freak friends, probably."

Lily was still watching the girl walk away and so was I. "I didn't want a trick from her," Lily said.

124

I hugged her. I was always hugging Lily. I had gotten it into my mind that I might be able to get her to eat more if she had enough touch. Maybe I just needed it, too. "You're right," I said. But I didn't tell them how I knew she was—I recognized the girl.

We went inside. None of us felt like doing anything after that. Together they took turns painting my face white with a black triangle over my nose, black slashes around my mouth, and black hollows around my eyes to look like a skull. It was how I felt, but the touch of the makeup brush was soothing, tender, just a little ticklish. We ate 3 Musketeers bars (or Bobby and I did), watched *Addams Family* and *Twilight Zone* reruns on TV, and fell asleep in a heap on my bed. We didn't talk about what had happened and I was grateful. I was glad they were there.

A few days later I got up the courage to knock on Winter's door. It was afternoon and the sun was shining but the air was chilly. I stood shivering on his doorstep, waiting. This time I didn't just have his sister and his dogs and a confrontation with his mother to be afraid of. Staci might be with him and I'd have to face the fact that they were actually together.

After a long time he answered. He was wearing a

dirty T-shirt and rumpled jeans, rubbing his eyes as if he'd been sleeping. He just stared at me.

"Do you even know who I am?" I said.

It took a while for him to answer. "That Bat girl, right? I think I know your dad or something? Are you here to see Anna?"

"Winter!" I raised my voice this time. "What are you doing? What's wrong with you?"

He ran a hand through his greasy hair. There were dark circles under his eyes like the ones my friends and I had painted on for Halloween.

"Is she home?" I asked, more softly. "Your sister?"

"No. I don't know where she goes. She takes the dogs and goes out for hours."

"How about your girlfriend, Staci?"

"Staci." He smiled like a five-year-old who had just received some candy. Then he looked worried. "She's not here."

"What about your mom?" This time I would give the purple lady a piece of my mind.

I brushed past Winter. He didn't stop me.

I went into his sister's room and looked around. A pink dress was tossed over a chair and a mannequin head with a blonde wig was on the dressing table next to a black-and-white photo of the '50s actress Jayne

Mansfield. I noticed there were other photos of her on the walls, next to pictures of James Dean, Sal Mineo, Marilyn Monroe, and a dancer I recognized as Isadora Duncan, the one who died when her flowing scarf got caught in the wheel of the car she was driving in. A black pillowcase lay on the floor, overflowing with candy bars.

I went to the dressing table. Two dolls were seated on it. The Barbie had a hard, simpering smile on her little face and hard plastic breasts jutting out under her striped sweater. She was holding a small chain, like the ones we all wore around our necks then, dangling with gold charms. The chain was fastened around the neck of the Ken doll that sat beside her. He was tall and blonde. He had a small, black blindfold covering his eyes.

I ran out of the room and found Winter lying on his bed staring at the ceiling. I grabbed his hand and he got up slowly.

"Look!" I shouted at him, dragging him into his sister's room. "Don't you see what she's doing?"

Winter looked around at the pictures of dead stars, at the spilled candy and the wig and the dolls. Nothing registered in his eyes.

That was when I heard the door open and the sound

of the dogs scrambling in. They appeared at the bedroom door, growling, with the girl behind them.

"What is she doing in my room?" She was talking to her brother but her eyes were fiercely locked on me as if she could keep me from moving with her stare. It worked. She was wearing the puffed sleeved dress and her saddle shoes. I saw one of the dog's black lips curl so that its teeth showed.

I looked at Winter and something changed in his eyes. He commanded the dogs to go to their beds and took me by the arm.

"She was just leaving," he said.

Annabelle watched us go. She had the same snarl on her mouth as her chow had worn. I wondered who had thought of it first.

At the door I turned to Winter and held his wrist with both my hands. "Please," I said. "Please come talk to me."

The look of recognition and concern was gone. He slipped out of my grip and stared down at the ground, rolling onto the outer edges of his feet. That was how he remained, standing like that in the doorway of number 13, as I left him.

Bobby wasn't good at keeping his mouth shut and I loved that about him and because of it I especially loved how he had avoided talking to me about Winter, even after the weirdness he had witnessed. Finally, though, after that last visit, I told him and Lily the whole story, except the part about my dad. I just said that Winter had happened to be protective of me in those situations with his sister and Staci.

"It sounds wicked to me," Bobby said. We were sitting at our usual lunch spot and I wanted him to lower his voice in case someone heard. "All of it. I'd avoid them all if I were you."

Lily was watching me intently. "It's not that easy, Bobby." She gave him a meaningful look that was supposed to convey something along the lines of *She's got a huge crush on the guy, you dork*, but he ignored it. Well, mostly.

"Foxiness is as foxiness does," he said, so I guess he did get what she was saying. "We need to find you someone better to crush on."

"It's not that! I don't *like* like him. I just think something really weird is going on."

"Obviously weird shit is happening but we don't need to get involved. Let them voodoo themselves to death. What do you care?" Bobby took a bite out of his bologna sandwich, made a face, and tossed it into the trash bin.

I stared at my checkerboard Vans. They were the same ones Winter wore.

"She cares," Lily said, clutching her apple.

So Bobby dropped the subject. I guess the look on my face was clear enough.

I really didn't want to get involved. I wanted to walk away from the whole thing. Winter and Staci and the creepy sister and the purple-eyed betrayer. I had enough to worry about. But it was more complicated than that. Annabelle had seen me in her room. She'd already attacked me for less.

The next few days I walked around like a hunted deer, perking up my ears, startling at every loud sound, flashing my gaze in every direction. I almost wished she'd show up, just to get it over with. But she never came.

Not much happened at all. My mom continued to sit around watching TV and drinking. A couple of times I tried to ask her if she had any idea what the notes I'd gotten meant or who she thought had sent them but she told me she had no idea what I was talking about and once actually started whistling.

She went out, disguised as much as possible in huge sunglasses and a head scarf—only to cash the checks she received in the mail so I could use them to buy groceries. The checks were from my dad but there was never a return address or even a note in them.

He didn't call. I kept expecting him to call and he didn't and finally I stopped jumping every time the phone rang.

Winter and Staci hung out and he always had the same blank expression on his face.

I spent as much time as possible with Bobby and Lily. It was the only way I felt halfway okay. Luckily, we all felt like that, so none of us noticed or at least minded the desperate way we clung to each other.

I found out more about them. Bobby's mother never came home when we were over there but his sister was a skinny, brown-skinned blonde with a shag haircut who grunted at us when she got home, went into her bedroom, and shut the door. He rolled his eyes and called her Miss Mean Jeans. They had different dads and neither had bothered to stick around. I got the feeling that Bobby's mother did something illegal for a living but he never really said. I'd seen her picture—blonde hair like the sister, giant breasts, and the same green cat eyes as Bobby. He said his father was a Mexican drug lord but I had no idea if it was true. Bobby always had new clothes and albums and sometimes pot and I wondered where he got the money for that but he just shrugged, batted his cartoon eyelashes, and looked mysterious when I hinted that he must have a pretty big allowance or a secret job he wasn't telling us about.

Lily was the stable one in our group, we joked, because she still had two parents living at home and the home was an actual house. The reason it was a joke, though, of course, was that Lily was just as messed up as Bobby and me, maybe more so because she never ate. Her father was a dentist who washed his hands a hundred times a day and her mother was a professional housewife who liked to cook elaborate meals to entice her daughter into eating. The huge, fatty dishes only made Lily starve herself more. It turned out that the lasagna story was true. Someone must have heard her mother telling the school counselor about it because it got around and she'd never been able to escape. She told me that sometimes she dreamed about her mom's dinners coming to life—headless zombie chickens and chocolate cakes oozing fat—and chasing her, trying to choke her to death.

"Have you ever gotten help?" I finally asked. I knew I should have said it before but I was scared it might make things worse.

"My mom made me see this shrink once," she told us. "And then I started group therapy with all these other girls but it just gave me more ideas about how to lose weight so they pulled me out. I'd hide in the bathroom with the door locked during my shrink sessions so they finally gave up but I have to weigh myself every morning and if I go below ninety I have to go to a hospital."

"Sweetie," I said, hugging her. I wanted to make her soup but I was a lousy cook and I knew she didn't want any either.

Bobby didn't say anything. He went into the kitchen and came back with a large green apple and a cup of peppermint tea with lemon and honey.

I was thinking a lot about my friends those days and not so much about my family or my neighbors.

But one night it happened.

I got home late from the store. It was dark early—we'd just put the clocks back. My arms were full of groceries and I was starving. I'd spent the afternoon at Bobby's and come home to find that we didn't have anything to eat in the house.

As I was walking through the gate I heard whispering from the shadows. I stopped.

"Don't you dare go any farther," the voice said.

Annabelle jumped out from behind the low stucco

wall. She was wearing the blonde wig, the long, pink satin dress, and loads of costume jewelry. Compared to her, Staci, Marci, and Kelli look like kittens with bells on their collars trying to chase birds.

"What the hell?" I stepped back and almost tripped.

"What the hell is right? What the hell were you doing in my room?" she spat.

"I was visiting your brother." You know how they say it feels like your heart is in your mouth? That.

"My brother doesn't want to see you in our house either," the girl said.

The eggs were rattling in the bag I held. I wondered if they would break. I tried to get my hands to stop shaking. She's just a girl, I told myself.

It didn't help.

"What did you buy?" she asked, her voice shrill.

She grabbed one of the grocery bags out of my hands and opened it. I just stood there. I felt like Winter when he looked at Staci, like I couldn't even move.

Annabelle took out the carton of eggs I had just bought. She opened the container carefully and examined them.

"Stop it," I said, but weakly. I wanted to make pancakes, bacon, and scrambled eggs for dinner. Sometimes it cheered me up to eat meals at the "wrong times." Maybe my mom would eat some, too.

"Always check for cracked ones," she said softly. She was whistling to herself or maybe to the eggs in the carton. "You don't want any cracked ones, you know. Are any of you cracked, little chicken fetuses?"

Then she looked up at me and her eyes were glittering. I mean, her eyes were actually lit up with tiny sparks of hate like black water in the sunlight. She started hurling the eggs at me. I put my hands over my face as the eggs slammed into me, drenching me in gooey streams of phlegmy yolk.

"Stop it!" I screamed. "Stop it! Who are you? Get away from me!"

She wouldn't stop. I crouched into a little ball on the ground, covering my head with my arms as the eggs cracked, every last one. I didn't run. There was nowhere to go. I screamed but I didn't scream for help. In that moment I had decided not to. I knew no one would come.

If my guardian angel heard me he had decided not to bother. He was busy with Staci Nettles.

When every last egg was gone the girl walked away. I got up, gathered the remaining groceries, and went inside. My mom was asleep in front of the TV. I took a shower and put away the food. I couldn't eat anything.

I went and lay on my bed, staring at the ceiling until I fell asleep. I didn't even have the fantasy of Winter to comfort me anymore.

It was late for anyone to call us. I woke right away but stared at the phone in shock for the first three rings before I pounced. It was him.

I started sobbing as soon as I heard his voice. "Where are you? You didn't even give me a phone number. It's been two months! Two months. How could you do that to us?"

"I had to straighten some things out," he said when I stopped. "I'm sorry. I didn't know when to call, if she'd answer."

"What are you afraid of? Of Mom? You left me here with this insane neighbor. She threw eggs and sicced her dogs on me! Who is she? Her mother has your picture!" I was shrieking now, my voice getting louder and louder and suddenly I stopped, afraid he'd hang up, but he was still there.

"Weetzie. Stop. Stop. What are you talking about? You're not making sense."

I gulped for air. "The daughter of your *friend*. Winter's sister. She's a psycho. And someone keeps giving me these notes."

"Slow down, honey. I don't understand."

"I think she put a curse on him or something." I started crying again and he mumbled softly to me until I quieted down.

"Weetzie," he said. "Baby." I loved the tobacco corduroy sound of his voice. "I really don't know what you're telling me. Who are these people?"

"Stop denying it!"

"Honey," he said patiently, "I'm not denying anything."

I gulped down tears. Was he telling the truth? Was it possible he didn't know? That Winter had made it all up? That *I* had made it all up—even Winter?

"I'll be back around Thanksgiving, okay? That's not that far away. I'll take you to dinner. The Tick Tock. We'll have pressed turkey and cranberry jelly and pumpkin pie under the cuckoo clocks, okay? It'll be okay. I'll give you my phone number. I have a place now. It's kind of small but you can come visit me sometime and we'll walk the whole length of the city from downtown up and back. I love you, baby."

I didn't say anything. I didn't want him to talk to Winter. I wanted him to talk to me—I wanted him to come back.

"Did you hear me, baby?"

"Yes, Daddy."

"Can I sing to you?" he asked.

I was lying in bed now with my damp head and my tears making a huge wet spot on the pillow, the phone pressed to my cheek. It was almost as if he were there with me. His rough voice sang the lullaby from my childhood, just like he used to sing when I was tucked into my bed in the cottage.

"Under Baby's cradle in the night/Stands a goat so soft and snowy white/The Goat will go to the market/To bring you wonderful treats/He'll bring you raisins and almonds/Sleep, my little one, sleep."

The exhaustion of the whole day hit me like one of the hurled eggs and I cowered into the blankets and closed my eyes.

When I woke up the receiver was still pressed against my hot ear. I realized I hadn't gotten his phone number after all.

A few days later I was leaving school with my friends when I saw Winter's VW Bug pull up and park in the loading zone.

He got out of the car. I watched as Staci went to him with a confident smirk and hair toss.

She stepped in front of him and put her hand on his arm. He spoke quietly to her and then moved his arm away. It was a cool day and he had on gray Levi's cords and a white, long-sleeved thermal shirt under a hooded sweatshirt. He looked up and even from that far away I could see how blue his eyes were. He was looking at me.

Staci watched him as he came over to me. Suddenly, I noticed how short she was, even in her superhigh platforms. She didn't even bother to toss her hair. She just walked away.

"Weetzie," Winter said.

I looked at Lily and then at Bobby, trying to figure out what I was supposed to do.

"I have to go to the 7-Eleven," Bobby said. "Slurpee withdrawal. We'll meet you at your house in like an hour?"

"Yeah," Lily said.

They walked away. Shit.

I started to follow them—"Guys!"—but Winter stopped me.

"Are you okay?" he asked.

I shrugged. "Why do you care? You've been acting like you don't even know who I am."

"Will you let me give you a ride home? I want to explain it. Please."

I felt like flipping him off but instead I just started walking.

"I'm going to get a parking ticket. Please, Weetzie."
Then he added, "Let me explain."

That was what got me—I followed him.

I sat in his car with my arms folded on my chest. The Bug smelled of sawdust. He leaned over and buckled me in. I breathed the clean, herbal scent of his hair over the dry undertones of the Bug's stuffing. I kicked at the floorboards, pressing my feet down as hard as I could. We didn't say anything to each other for a long time.

"Listen, I want to explain something," he said, finally. "My sister has a serious problem."

"I kind of got that."

"I'm not trying to make excuses but she's had this . . . influence over me. She does this thing and I start acting really weird. It's happened before. Around Halloween, especially. I didn't think she could do it anymore but I guess I was wrong."

I turned to look at him. "What are you talking about? You sound like a crazy person. You're as bad as she is."

He pulled over and parked the car. Everything looked especially bleak in the gray weather. L.A. wasn't made for days like this. Even the buildings and the pavement, embedded with sparkling bits, needed sun in order not to look depressed.

"I know it sounds freaky. Maybe I am crazy, I don't know. But my sister does these things, these spells. And I guess the last one worked on me. She got me to hang out with Staci and I know Staci was a bitch to you and that I acted like a shit, too. I'm really sorry."

"Why the sudden change of heart?" I said grandly. I had heard my mom say that to my dad once. I thought it sounded like a line in a movie or at least a daytime soap opera.

I saw him repress a small smile. Then he looked serious again. I hated how cute he was.

"I spoke to Charlie about it."

"My dad says he doesn't know you. Who are you all? What do you have to do with my father? And what are those notes about? I got another one. Just leave us alone!"

I tried to get out of the car but he leaned over and stopped me. The blonde hairs on his tan arms shone softly even on that sunless day. His mouth was close to mine—I could see the slightly chapped skin on his lower lip—and for a second I had the strangest feeling that he wanted to kiss me. It can't be real though, I told myself. You're hallucinating, Weetzie Bat.

"Your dad really loves you," Winter said. "Just remember that, okay? You're lucky to have a father who loves you so much."

Then he moved his arm and let me go out into the glitter-less cold.

THE MAGIC OF FORGETTING

$\mathcal{M}$y dad did come a few days before Thanksgiving like he said he would. He was waiting for me, down the street from the Starlight, when I got home from school, sitting parked in the bashed-up yellow T-bird that he had crashed once while making out with my mother as they drove down PCH to watch the sun set at the beach. We had agreed not to tell my mom that he was coming. He looked thinner and paler than when he had left and he still had the five o'clock shadow all over his chin. I thought of how many times it must have been shaved off and sprouted back since I'd last seen him. He got out of the car and held me and I wanted to melt into the warmth of his tweedy arms, become part of him so that he would never be able to leave me. It seems impossible that you can love one person so much, no matter what happens, no matter what they do. How just a lullaby or a turkey dinner can make up for so much in the moment. And how you can keep looking for someone like that person for the rest of your life. I knew then that that is what I would always be doing—looking for a Charlie Bat, for his lullabies and his dinners and his smell and his coats. He put one arm around my shoulders and looked into my face. He had tears in his eyes and I thought about how sometimes he started crying when he read me bedtime stories like *Peter Pan* or *The Wizard of Oz* and how it made my stomach feel weird and ticklish in a bad way to see him like that.

"Are you eating, skinny bones?"

"You should talk." I squeezed his bicep.

"Well, you look cute skinny. But I think we both need a good Tick Tock cooked meal."

Going out to eat was one of our favorite things to do together. When I was little he liked to take me to Norms Coffee Shop for hamburgers and vanilla shakes that we ate in the vinyl booths, or we went to Ships where you could make your own toast in the toasters at your table. We had ice-cream cones at Wil Wright's ice-cream parlor in Hollywood, with the striped awning and the parquet floor. We drove all the way out to the Valley to Farrell's where they made a huge ice-cream birthday concoction called the Zoo that was covered with little plastic animals. The waiters, dressed in boater hats, striped shirts, and suspenders, ran around the restaurant honking horns until they arrived at your table to sing "Happy Birthday." There was also something called a Trough that was so big you became an honorary pig for the night if you ate it all by yourself.

The Tick Tock didn't have Zoos or Troughs but we went there a lot, too. There were cuckoo clocks all over the walls. I wondered who had invented the cuckoo clock. There was something so weird about that little wooden cuckoo popping out of its house every hour.

Charlie escorted me inside and we sat down under the wooden birds and ate the orange sticky buns the restaurant was famous for, as well as turkey dinners with pressed turkey and cranberry jelly and mashed potatoes. We didn't say much to each other through dinner. I kept thinking of things I wanted to ask, and then stopping myself because I was afraid that if I asked it might drive him away even farther and sooner.

Why did you leave?

Why did you and Mom fight?

Why did you go to New York?

Why do you like it better there?

Do you have new friends?

Do you miss us?

Who is the family in number 13?

I didn't ask any of these questions so there was kind of a tense silence through our meal. My dad asked me about school and my friends and how the dog walking was going but he avoided anything about my mom or what I had said during our last phone conversation. I ate too much and my stomach hurt, pressing against the tight waistband of my high-rise jeans.

Finally, I said, "Dad, tell me the truth."

He put down his fork and wiped his mouth. "What do you want to know?"

"Were you having an affair? Is that the reason you and Mom fought?"

"We've had troubles for years, your mother and I, Weetzie, you know that."

I pulled apart an orange sticky roll. My fingers were glossy with sugar. "But never this bad."

He nodded and reached across the table to cup my

hand under his. My whole hand disappeared. "Let's not talk about this anymore. I just want to enjoy our time together."

And, just like that, easy as pie, I fell for it again. It was the same as the lullaby and the dinner and the jacket, dense and tweedy with a world of warmth and comfort inside its lining. His hand on my hand was all I really cared about then. When I got out of the car he gave me a bouquet of pink roses he had hidden in the backseat. I didn't have to hide them from my mom— she was passed out when I got home.

My dad took me out again the next day and we went shopping at a mall. I don't know how he had the money but I didn't question it. He bought me some Clinique face powder and blush in their little pale-green marbled plastic cases and a bottle of Jontue perfume with the unicorn on the box. He even bought me a new pair of Kork-Ease since the pale suede soles of mine were dirty and the beige leather straps had turned a soiled dark brown. They weren't the really high ones but they weren't the almost-flat ones either. I felt greedy, like I wanted to gather up every last bit of pretty to remind me that he had been here, that he cared. In the same way I ate a double-scoop pistachio-and-cherry ice-cream cone and then had popcorn and a large Sprite at the movie theater where we saw *Young Frankenstein* for the second time. My dad guffawed but I just sat there chomping on popcorn and rolling my eyes along with Igor. But still I wanted more. I didn't want it to be over. After the movie we went to Café Figaro for dinner. It was dark and there was sawdust on the floors and we ate bread and soup and the waiters were very beautiful young men in white button-down shirts. My dad and I didn't talk about anything serious. By then I realized that it would only make things harder when he left.

We drove home along Santa Monica Boulevard. Something flashed in my eye and my mind and I put my head out the window and looked behind us at the boy I'd seen. I almost told my dad to stop but something in me hesitated because I didn't want it to be him.

"What?" Charlie asked.

"I thought I recognized someone. A friend from school."

"Out here? I hope not. No kids should be out here at night."

I looked at the men in tight pants and small, cropped beards walking along the boulevard, the boys loitering under the streetlights, a strange, alien glitter streaking off of them like pretty, used cars in a nighttime car lot. I had a brief fantasy of bringing them all home with me and feeding them alphabet soup while my mom yelled for more gin from the sofa.

But had I really seen Bobby Castillo among them? My Bobby wearing a short-sleeved pink polo shirt and Top-Siders I'd never seen (that proved it wasn't him, right?), his curls lusciously rebellious in contrast to his clothes? I closed my eyes, my head still out the window, and let the night exhale across my face, blowing away the vision of my friend.

When my dad dropped me off I took my new things out of the bag and held them and smelled them—lilies and leather—until I fell asleep.

The senses can give you magical gifts, no matter what else is happening. Especially if you know how to use them selectively.

I was learning.

He came to see me one last time before he left. He pulled up and stopped the car but he didn't get out. I went over to him and he reached into the seat beside him and picked something up in his hands. It was tiny and it wiggled and yapped. I saw petal ears, a pointy nose, and the brightest black eyes. The slinky body squirmed free from his hands and into mine, and the cold, wet nose began to nuzzle my neck and armpit as if it were looking for milk.

"This is Monroe," he said. "She is to keep you company while I am gone."

A puppy should not be an excuse for leaving. Just as ice cream or perfume or roses or the pink rhinestone collar twinkling around Monroe's wrinkly neck weren't. None of it should have been an excuse but I allowed it to be.

Monroe's little heart thrummed under the thin membrane of her skin. She nipped gently at my fingers with her needle teeth. I wanted to dress her up like a baby in a bonnet and roll her around in one of my old doll strollers. I wanted her to sleep in my bed, so the empty feeling that came every night when I turned out the lights would go away. I wanted to feed her puppy chow and take her for walks and clean up her poop with a pooper-scooper. I had been asking my parents for a puppy since I was three and the answer had always been no, so now, as I held her, I felt like a little kid again.

"What will Mom say?"

"Tell her you won her and a lifetime supply of pet food? I'll send you some money for it. Tell her she can't turn a hot dog named after her idol out on the street."

"A hot dog? Is she a wiener dog?"

"What d'ya think I am, a Chihuahua? A

Pomeranian?" he quipped in the voice of an incensed puppy. "I'm purebred as the driven snow and don't you forget it!"

"Does she have all her shots?"

"Yep. But she hasn't had any of those brutal operations yet, so make sure you keep her away from any big bad boy dogs in the neighborhood, until you're both ready for pups. And the same for you I might add, young lady."

"Dad!"

"Sorry. I just want to make sure your mother is sober enough to be able to explain about those birds and bees."

"I'm old enough to know about that!" I gave him a disgusted look and he smiled sheepishly.

"Sorry. I forget. You're a young lady now. But that's exactly why I worry."

Then I did what kids always do when they want to be comforted by a parent who can't really do it for them—I comforted him, even though what I was thinking was, If you don't want me to go boy crazy, why tell the cutest one in the neighborhood to keep an eye on me? "We'll take care of each other," I said. "Right, Monroe?"

Well, we had to. Charlie was not going to do it for us.

"Hey, Dad," I said. "What about all those notes I keep finding? Do you know anything about that?"

"What notes?" he asked.

"The Max Factor museum? The tar pits? A mime gave me one."

"A mime? You should ask that guy in the building. What's his name? Hoople something? He's a mime."

Monroe whimpered. It was pointless. "Never mind."

"I have to leave you now, ladies," he said softly, stepping out of the car and putting his arms around us. Monroe, pressed closer against me, stuck out her tongue as if I'd pushed a button, and licked my face. She felt warm but the day had grown cold. I thought of going in and calling Bobby and Lily. I hadn't seen them all weekend. I would show them Monroe and make hot chocolate with whipped cream and mini marshmallows for us to share. I was starting to learn how to forget the things that made me sad. It was like a charm you followed step-by-step, collecting and blending the ingredients, placing everything in its proper place, reciting the incantation. It was the magic of forgetting.

WINTER IN L.A.

After my dad left I thought things might settle down a little. I had my friends and a sweet dog and I knew, or at least thought, my father would come back again eventually. School was boring but not as traumatic as it had been. Casey, Jeff, and Rick were sobered by the acne incident even though Casey's face had cleared up. Marci and Kelli seemed to have lost interest in us.

But there was still the mystery of the notes I'd

received. I was no closer to solving the second one. (Ben Hoopleson had not been any help at all. Basically you can't get much information out of a mime.) And there was still Staci. Winter had dumped her and I was the person he had gone to that day when she waited for him in front of the school.

"Hey, Louise!" she called. I was lacing up my skates after school waiting for Bobby and Lily.

"I need to talk to you."

I squinted up at her, shielding my eyes. The sun was out again and it was harsh even though the air felt a little cold. Goose bumps studded my arms like armor.

"Yeah?" I snapped a decent-sized bubble at her but she ignored it.

"If you think that Wiggins has any interest in you, you're wrong. He told me what he thinks about you."

I stood up to face her. My legs were shaking in the skates and I had to hold on to the stair railing. Low blood sugar, I told myself. I wanted to scream at her but my throat felt like I had swallowed a tablespoon of sand.

I felt warm fingers on my arm and turned to see Bobby standing there. Lily was behind him.

"You okay?" Bobby asked. Suddenly, because they were there, I was.

"I was just warning the queen of the geeks here to stay away from my boyfriend."

"He's not your boyfriend," I said. "Staci Nettles, he has no feelings for you whatsoever."

She looked shocked for a second, then flipped her hair as if to restore her confidence. The long strands fell back in place in a perfect golden cascade.

"He told me how your dad paid him to watch out for you and how you tried to make a pass at him. You're completely gross."

Then she walked away and I leaned against Bobby. "Paid him!"

"Wow," he said. "She won't quit, will she?"

"Someday I'm going to figure out what to say to her to make her stop," I told them, but they both looked at me skeptically and I wondered if I was wrong.

One night I heard my mom talking in her sleep. I went over and stroked her hair and told her she was dreaming but she kept mumbling. I leaned closer to make out the words.

"Tell that woman to leave! She's ruined my life. Tell her to go away! She's caused enough damage. Why does she have to stay in our house? Tell her to leave."

"Mom?" I said softly. "Mom?"

155

"Tell her to leave."

"I know," I said. "I know how hard this is. Everything will be okay." I didn't know if that was true but it seemed like the thing to murmur when someone you loved was having a nightmare. Maybe I would go and tell Purple Eyes to leave whether my dad admitted to her existence or not. I had to gather my strength for it. Not only was she scary as heck, I wasn't even sure if she was real or I had made her up in my crazy mind, along with Annabelle and Winter and the notes.

Then one night as I was coming home alone from Bobby's house, I felt someone grab me from behind and pull me into the stairwell. The small fingers covered my mouth as I struggled to break free. I knew who it was.

If Winter was my guardian angel, what was Annabelle? The thought made me nauseous and dizzy with fear.

She moved her hand and I whirled to face her—she held me only with her gaze. Her eyes were glossy, blank, unseeing. Her fingers were moving, the thumb of each hand tapping the other four fingers in succession and then again.

I could have run but I didn't. I just stared at her.

My limbs felt like bags of sand.

"Your father left you. Your mother leaves every time she takes a drink. Your friends will go away, too. All I see ahead for you is darkness."

"Stop!" I screamed. "Stop it! It's not true! That's not what life is! Why do you hate me so much?"

"I'm just a reflection of how you feel about yourself."

"No," I said. "No you're not." I straightened out my spine and looked into her eyes. "I like myself now. No matter what my parents do, it doesn't mean that I'm not a good person or even that they don't love me."

"But they're gone," she said.

"Not all the way. They love me the best they can. And besides," I said, my voice breaking, but only a little, "I can take care of myself if I have to. I can take care of myself and other people, too, and I am going to be okay."

She seemed to evaporate then, because the next moment she had slipped out of my grasp and was gone. The pool was dazzling blue under the lights through the gate. It looked as if mermaids cut silver paths beneath the surface. There was a fat, mottled moon in the sky. The air smelled of flowers and citrus, even though it was nearing winter. *It's never winter in Los*

Angeles. No matter what the little witch said, I knew love was real and I knew I was loved. Even if I had to mostly just love myself. Why else were we here except to love?

There was one thing more I had to do. *You must not be afraid,* the man in the turban had said. It had taken me a while to understand but I thought I finally did, not just with my head but with my heart.

Every night for a week I checked the parking space for number 13 and when I finally saw a black Porsche I went and knocked on the door. This time the woman answered. Her hair fell around her shoulders and her face was pale without makeup. She wore a silk kimono covered with large, red poppies and her feet were bare, the nails a little long and painted crimson. I felt suddenly cold when I looked at her and I wished I had brought Monroe to keep me warm, but of course, I couldn't have because of the dogs. They stood behind her in the darkened room, growling.

"Yes?" she asked. Her voice, even with the heavy, warm accent, sounded as cold as my goose-bumped arms felt.

"I need to talk to you," I said. "About Charlie."

"Who are you?"

"You know who I am. I'm his daughter. May I come in?"

She shook her head. "I'm sorry. That's impossible." She started to shut the door and I wedged myself in so she couldn't.

"I talked to Annabelle. She told me who she is."

"Annabelle has issues," the woman said. "She isn't well. You can't listen to what she says."

"Then help her," I told her. "I don't want to hear her stories about my dad and I don't want her to attack me with those dogs or anything else. You need to control her. Winter can't do it alone. She messes with him, too. She made him into a zombie or something."

She looked as if she were going to slap me across the face the way they do in soap operas with one long, graceful, disdainful smack.

I didn't flinch, though. I said, "If you don't want to hear the truth from me you might as well just move away. My dad's not here anymore. He's never coming back. Maybe he left because of us but maybe he left because of you and there's no reason for you and your family to stay here anymore and make us miserable."

I don't know where that voice came from. It was so

much stronger than I was but it wasn't me pretending to be someone else, someone in a movie, someone who was confident and sure of herself. It was my voice.

I moved away from the door frame and she slammed the door shut.

Inside the rooms I would never enter again was a photograph of my father with the woman who lived there. There was also, somewhere behind that door, a boy who had saved me more than once and more than he knew.

The next day I went to a craft store and bought a rhinestone gun and multicolored rhinestones, a bag of pink feathers, and as many fake flowers as I could afford. I gunned rhinestones and sewed flowers and glued feathers all over every piece of old clothing I owned. It might just seem like silly fashion but it mattered. It mattered because I believed it did.

When it got dark I went out and picked a bag full of flowers from the neighborhood gardens. I filled all my mom's empty liquor bottles with bouquets. Some of the roses were as big as my face. The pale yellow ones smelled like lemons, the purple ones smelled like lavender, and the orange ones smelled like honey. This mattered, too.

In the morning I went to the grocery store and bought ingredients to make pasta with pesto sauce and a spinach salad with walnuts and dried cranberries and balsamic vinegar from a recipe I'd found in the one old cookbook that hadn't been totally ruined in the fire when I was a kid. I found an old damask tablecloth and set the table with roses and candles and our best dishes. Then I put on a waiter jacket I had found in a thrift store and invited my mom to dinner. She wore a yellow dress and I put a rose in her hair. The TV stayed off that night and even though my mom drank too much wine and passed out on the couch at least she had filled her tummy with something good first. I took off her shoes and covered her with a blanket. Then I took the candles and roses into the bathroom and got in the tub with some bubbles and scattered petals. The empty feeling that was usually inside of me, like the dark space when the lights go out, wasn't there at all.

It was Christmas Eve and I had just gotten back from hanging out at Bobby's. I had promised my mom I'd spend the evening with her. I was going to make turkey sandwiches, green beans with candied almonds, yams with marshmallows, and cranberry sauce. There were a few twinkle lights strewn over the roof of our building and the air smelled vaguely of fir trees and wood smoke. I thought, if you squint at the lights the right way they look beautiful, like magic. I had put a strand of battery-operated Christmas lights around my neck and they made the rhinestones on my jean jacket sparkle.

That was when I saw Hypatia's Porsche driving away with a moving trailer attached to the back and I ran up the stairs to number 13. I peeked into the unit and the front room was completely empty. Even the curtains were gone. It was as if no one had been there at all.

As I was walking away I heard my name and turned around.

Winter was standing in the empty living room. I had no idea where he'd come from. I took one look at him and realized something that had been heavy and growing in my heart since I'd first seen him. Whatever love meant there was some version of it that I felt for Winter. And it didn't matter if he felt that for me or not or if it was real love or just my sadness about my dad that had turned into longing. Love, that elusive leading lady, plays too many parts to be typecast. Winter was my first love—if you didn't count the moment I curled my newborn fingers around Charlie's index finger and gazed up into his eyes—and he was moving away from me, too.

"You scared me!" I said.

"I stayed to say good-bye to this place. I always have this little ritual when we move, where I say good-bye to everything but I realized there is nothing to say good-bye to here. Nothing that mattered."

We stood staring at each other and finally I couldn't stand it—something was welling up in my chest, ready to burst. It wasn't anger but I made it into that.

"My dad *paid* you to look out for me?" I said. I hadn't been able to get the thought out of my mind since Staci told me and I was afraid to ask Charlie about it when he called.

"What?" Winter blinked at me. He looked as if he'd grown taller since I'd seen him last. "Of course not."

"That's what Staci Nettles said."

"Like she knows anything." He moved toward the doorway. He was carrying a small duffel bag and had a backpack on his shoulders.

"Charlie asked me to watch out for you, in his way, but I wanted to do it. Especially when I got to know you. It's what we're supposed to do."

"We?"

He winked but he wasn't smiling. "Guardians. Angels. Right?"

So he was my angel. And he was leaving me.

"Where are you going?" I asked.

"I'm not sure. Out of this city anyway. My mom and Annabelle took off and I couldn't deal with them anymore. Besides, I turned eighteen today."

"Happy birthday."

I wanted to ask if he would be okay, if I could do anything. Would he be alone for his birthday? I wanted to give him a Christmas/birthday present and make him dinner. I wanted him to come live with us.

"Winter," I said.

"Yeah."

"Welcome Beauty, banish fear."

"What?"

"Never mind. Thank you."

He nodded and moved closer. He smelled like sand and tar and wind, gasoline and sawdust and oranges. He smelled like Los Angeles.

"I don't know if I can do this myself," I said, meaning everything, meaning life.

"Yes you can. You can do anything you put your mind to. You just needed a little help through adolescence, which just basically sucks for everyone, even if their parents are sane."

I smiled in spite of myself. I could see my reflection in his eyes.

"I lied. There's one thing that mattered," he said. "Good-bye, Weetzie Bat."

Then he leaned over and kissed the top of my head, pressing his face into my hair for just a second longer than an older brother or a father would, I told myself, with more intensity than would, say, just any old guardian angel.

The Christmas lights around my neck flashed on and off, illuminating our faces.

"There's no winter in L.A.," he said softly and I wanted to point out the smell of pine trees and fires burning and the snow that frosted the distant mountains and the twinkling lights right in front of his eyes and the hot/cold peppermint of our mouths but I knew what he meant.

"Oh, and by the way, you might think I did the CPR on your mom that time, but you actually remembered more than you thought you did."

He smiled at me, a shimmer of light, and then he was gone.

Maybe he was real. Maybe I'd made him up. Either way, he didn't think I needed him anymore. Maybe he was right.

On New Year's Eve Bobby and Lily and I climbed onto the roof of my building and made a nest out of flannel sleeping bags. We lay with our heads on each other's stomachs and watched the fireworks explode above our heads—burning chrysanthemums and fire fountains and heart-popping cherry bombs and shooting stars. Lily had stolen a bottle from her parents and we drank the cold, bitter white wine from plastic cups and chewed Bubble Yum to take the edge off.

"My mom would shit," Lily said, giggling. "That's the best Chardonnay we've got."

"Chardonnay? Wow, fancy name. She should try it with a bubble-gum chaser," Bobby said, blowing his.

"Might cheer her up," I added, out-blowing him.

Even Lily took a sip and then stuck a piece of sugarfree gum in her mouth, working her jaw delicately, as if it hurt her.

The sky kept filling up with shiny things and I could feel Bobby's taut stomach rising and falling under me, and Lily's light head with the wisps of hair resting on my belly.

"Let's do this every year for the rest of our lives," I said, sitting up.

"Yeah," said Bobby, "to that." He sat up, too, and

held up his glass. So did Lily but I noticed that she hesitated for an extra second and she didn't speak.

"To that."

"And to L.A.," I said. "Where it's always warm enough to lie on a roof."

We raised our cups and the wine shone like gold in the chemical light, as if we had caught one of the falling firework stars in our plastic cups.

"And to winter," I said. "Which it never is."

There was a deep silence between us as if they were both holding their breath and I knew they were wondering if I was okay, if I was sad that Winter was gone. My head was feeling light and hot from the wine. In that moment I was all right. I had my friends. I liked to think that the pink polo shirt Bobby wore that night for the first time had nothing to do with the one I'd seen on the boy on Santa Monica Boulevard. I had seen Lily's teeth tenderly nursing one marshmallow from the bag we had brought up with us and I told myself she might be getting better.

"Hey," she said. "Guess what?"

We both looked over at her. I felt something clench inside my chest.

"My parents are moving."

"What?" Bobby and I said it together. I had the

ridiculous impulse to give her more marshmallows to eat—a few calories she needed, and if she were eating she wouldn't be able to say anything more.

"I have to go into this children's hospital in Colorado so my parents are moving there," she said calmly but her hands nervously stroked the little layer of fur that had grown protectively over her arms.

Bobby flung his arm around her tiny shoulders. "Are you shitting me, Chin? I'm not going back to that junior hellhole if you don't."

"You guys have each other," she said, trying to smile. Her braces caught the light and twinkled merrily. It made me even sadder to see that brightness. I thought, Someone else is leaving. Again.

But at least maybe Lily would gain weight. I had stopped really seeing how bad it was. I looked at her then. Her bones stuck out like weapons and her eyes were sinking into her head. Her hair fell out when she combed it—I'd seen her sparsely covered scalp where she made her part and her brush full of broken strands.

I cuddled up next to her on the other side. We sat like that for a long time as the fireworks ended and the moon appeared again, watching us warily like a friend who was about to go away.

• • •

That New Year's Day I woke up with my heart pounding. I put on clothes and ran downstairs to the trash bin. I don't even know why I did it. I opened the bin and looked inside.

There was a cardboard box shoved into one corner under some plastic trash bags. Sticking out of the top was a Malibu Ken and a Francie doll with her hair in a ponytail. They were bound and gagged. I took them out, oblivious to the rotting banana peels, chicken carcasses, and moldy bread. I carefully removed the bandages from their mouths and the string from their hands and feet. I took them upstairs and bathed them and put them in my room but it was too late.

After vacation I went back to school expecting to cling to Bobby like a baby blanket or stuffed animal but I wasn't that surprised to find he was gone. I thought he might be sick so I called him, but no one answered. I went by his apartment and his sister opened the door.

I realized I didn't even know what her voice sounded like. She never spoke to us when she was around. Her blonde hair had grown out of the shag and was up in two pigtails and she had an unfocused look in her eyes. Her tiny legs were squeezed into a pair of torn, faded jeans and her feet were bare. The room smelled of pot.

A boy was lounging on the couch behind her watching TV.

"Hey," I said. "Is Bobby around?"

"We don't know where he is," she said. "We think he went to find his dad."

I thought of the Malibu Ken and the Francie doll waiting in my room. If there had been a doll to represent me, Anna had taken it away with her.

I HEART L.A.

*N*ot much happened the rest of the semester. I vowed just to get through until the summer so I focused on my schoolwork and taking care of my mom and Monroe, who I walked with as many of the neighbor's dogs as I could round up. I also spent a lot of time working on new outfits and I even made some for other people. I sewed a black cotton shirt for Mr. Gibbous, using an old shirt of my dad's for the pattern—they were about the same size—and I put special lining under the armpits to absorb any extra perspiration. When I gave it to him he coughed and blushed and tried to suppress a smile. Miss Spinner got a T-shirt with a rhinestone heart on it and Mr. Adolf got one with a peace sign—not that I expected either of them to wear theirs but at least Miss Spinner thanked me really graciously. Mr. Adolf said, "Well, well, well," and cleared his throat—I guess he thought I was messing with him. I designed a new pantsuit for Mrs. Musso, made out of some linen fabric I found at a thrift store and she did wear that. Even Staci got something—a denim shirt that I appliquéd with butterflies and flowers. I put it in her gym locker when she wasn't looking and without a note saying who it was from but she never wore it as far as I knew.

Staci avoided me all semester, except to give me vicious looks when she passed me in the hall. On the last day of school she came up to me where I was sitting alone, wearing jeans and a T-shirt with one of my dad's ties and his vest that I had covered with rhinestones. My yearbook was on my lap. No one had signed it at all. I smiled at Staci—maybe she was going to ask me to sign hers and then I could have her sign mine. Maybe she was going to thank me for the shirt and we could make some kind of peace.

"What's it like not to have any friends, Louise?" she

said, knowing, without even looking, that the book was empty of scrawled messages telling me to stay as sweet as I was and have a good summer vacation.

"It kind of sucks," I said. "You should know."

"I don't think so. I have hundreds of signatures in here."

"Well, I'd rather not have any than have them because people are afraid of me," I said.

Staci stood there looking me up and down, her yearbook full of signatures balanced on her neat little hip. She was wearing a blue-and-white-striped tube top and jeans. "You're not, though?" she asked.

"Afraid of you? No. I have other things to be afraid of. Like the disease that might be killing Lily Chin or how dangerous it is for Bobby on the streets or if I'll ever see Winter again or if I made him up. I worry about my mom's drinking problem and if my father is okay. But mostly, now, I try not to be afraid of anything. Life is too cool, you know? Oh and by the way, I've been practicing. Do you know how big a bubble I can blow?"

She wrinkled her nose and curled her upper lip irately.

"Enough to blow you away, that's how big."

I took a pink pillow-shaped piece of bubble gum out of my pocket, stuck it in my mouth, chewed it, and blew without taking my eyes off of her. Staci spat her old gum onto the ground, took a new piece out of her jeans, unwrapped it aggressively, popped it in her mouth, chewed, and blew—a bigger bubble. I blew back, an even bigger one. She tried again, but her bubble was small and flaccid.

I was still waiting for my last bubble to pop— instead it sailed out of my mouth, toward Staci's face. She backed away in horror but then my bubble floated gently up into the smoggy blue sky like a pink balloon. Staci's eyes flashed a fury that obviously went way beyond the art of bubble blowing. Then she turned and walked away, her plastic comb sticking out of the back pocket of her skintight jeans like a weapon that could no longer harm me.

Weeks passed. A slow, friendless, fatherless summer spent alone at the pool. I had pretty much given up on a lot of things, including discovering the meaning of the note I'd received before Halloween, but when I got home one night, there was a message from my dad on the machine.

"Our movie's on at midnight, your time, if you want to see it. Don't think you've ever seen this one."

I was surprised because he didn't usually leave

messages. He and my mom still seemed to be ignoring each other. But this time he had left something that she might hear. And he had even called the movie "ours," meaning his and hers, I thought, since she was the star. *The Beast in the Garden*, produced by Irv Feingold, had bombed pretty badly so they didn't talk about it. For that reason, and because I was afraid his voice might upset her, I didn't play her the message.

But I did stay up until after she fell asleep and then I snuck into the living room in my pajamas, holding Mink and Petal Bug. I sat on the floor in front of the TV screen and let the images buzz and flicker their way into my brain. He was right—I hadn't seen this one.

My mom, looking very young, blonde, and voluptuous in a pink dress, played a girl named Isabella whose rich father goes on a business trip and stumbles upon the castle of a mysterious stranger. The stranger, hidden in shadows, tells the father he has to bring his daughter back to work for him as punishment for trespassing. The father refuses but the girl, fearing for his life, insists on going and runs away to the castle where she becomes friends with the man who will never show his face. Finally, she discovers that his name is Count *Muerte*, that he was badly burned in a fire and considers himself a monster. She falls in love with him anyway but in the end he dies and a handsome youth comes to the castle to carry her away on his white horse.

It was pretty obvious what this was based on, especially when the count refers to it just before he dies at the end.

Welcome Beauty, banish fear
You are queen and mistress here
Speak your wishes, speak your will
Swift obedience meets them still.

With that, I understood a lot of things but I still didn't know where the note wanted me to go.

Where I did go was into my room and got it out of the music box, read the ransom-style letters. Then I went and found the box full of my dad's old notebooks and looked through them until I came to an interview someone had done with him about *The Beast in the Garden*. The paper was yellowing and torn and the print faded but still readable.

In the interview, my dad said that my mom's character was based on "a famous actress whose name we won't mention here. Because she's the ultimate tortured beauty."

"Count *Muerte?*" the interviewer wrote. "Fairly obvious, wouldn't you say?"

"Death is always obvious," replied my father, "but that doesn't mean we ever get used to it, do we?"

The ultimate Beauty and the ultimate Beast, the ultimate Fear.

My movie queen and mistress here

I knew where to go. The next morning. On my birthday.

It was hidden away. You wouldn't even know it was there. You certainly wouldn't know, driving by, that a goddess's remains were there. My goddess.

I took the bus down Wilshire into Westwood, got out at Glendon, and wandered around for a while, trying to find the entrance to the park. Finally, a grumpy ticket-taker at the nearby theater pointed me across a plaza and down an alley that led to the gate of an old churchyard hidden among the high buildings. There was a drive that circled a plot of green planted with large trees. They spread their branches low as if they were trying to comfort you. I walked along the path to my left. Coming toward me were two people I recognized: Tom "Sunshine" Abernathy and Uncle Oz from the condos. They were walking arm in arm. Tom was wearing the blonde wig he had let me try on once, or one of them, and a long pink dress. He waved at me and Oz nodded and they kept strolling along, toward the entrance. I didn't have much time to ask them what they were doing there and I didn't really have to—it was the one day of the year when everyone came to pay their respects.

A small crowd of people were gathered at the crypt that was tucked unassumingly into a low wall in the shade. There were flowers everywhere—giant heart-shaped rose wreathes, little posies and nosegays and bouquets of all shapes and sizes. The stone was a light reddish color, from all the lipstick kisses of all the mourners for the last thirteen years. *Kiss your wishes.* I felt tears surge up in my chest and I had to keep myself from getting down on my knees and weeping. If you thought about her at all, no matter who you were, if you had any heart at all, it would make you cry. She was everything beautiful and sad in the world. She'd lost babies and husbands and she drank and took pills and she had light pouring out from under her skin like her spirit was too bright for one person's body, even a curva-ceously giving body like that. I would never be like her and I didn't even really want to be. I just wanted to let her know that everything I would do or be for the rest of my life was a way to honor her in some way, to let her know that things didn't have to end like that. I hoped they didn't. I wanted to prove her wrong. I loved her.

Charlie tells little Weetzie they are going somewhere special, somewhere magical. She is very excited—she dresses up in her best purple flowered dress and looks at herself in the mirror. Pretty!

Charlie drives her in the Thunderbird. This is before she knows the layout of the city, before she thinks of it as her city. It is just a big place that her parents understand but she doesn't. There are nice things about it—places with twinkling lights and tinkling music, but she doesn't know how to get to any of them.

At first this place just looks like a gate and then it looks like a park without swing sets or anything fun and then she sees the plaques in the ground and realizes what it really is. And she starts to cry.

"Why did you bring me here?"

It is worse than the mama elephant sinking into tar.

He picks her up, apologizing, but he won't leave. He wants to show her something.

"See," he says. "This is her grave. People from all over the world come to worship her. See the roses? See the kisses?"

179

Weetzie wants more than a cold stone with roses and kisses. She wants Marilyn Monroe to be alive, like she is alive, like her mom, like her dad. She tells him that.

"She's more alive than I am," says her father.

"Marilyn," I said, kissing the marble even though my lip gloss was too light to make much of a mark, more of a gloppy pale-pink smudge.

Among all the little notes tucked along the edges, there was an envelope taped to the stone and I recognized it right away. It was silver and had my name written on it. Inside there was glitter but no note. Just a plane ticket to New York City.

"You're never coming back, Louise!" my mom said, clinking the ice in her glass. I had told her I wanted to visit my dad in New York.

"Mom, my name is not Louise." I spoke softly, the way you would to a child.

She swiped at a tear from her eye like a cat catching a spider. "I'm a terrible mother."

"No you're not. Stop that. Just call me by my name."

"You're never coming back."

"I promise I will," I told her. "It's just for a few weeks. I'll call you every day."

Just then Monroe, as if on cue, jumped up onto her lap and began licking her face. My mom pretended to be annoyed, "Get that dog off," but her posture softened and she held Monroe's body gently in both hands, close to her bosom, almost like you would hold a baby.

"She's excited to be spending special time with Grandma, right, Monroe? Right, little starlet?"

"Don't leave us alone too long, my Weetzie," my mother said, and I knew that was her way of giving me her blessing.

She never called me Louise again after that.

He met me at LaGuardia in a short-sleeved white shirt and black trousers. His back was wet with sweat when he hugged me.

"So you found the ticket?"

"The notes were all from you?"

"Merrily the feast I'll make/Today I'll brew, tomorrow bake/Merrily I'll dance and sing for next day will a stranger bring/Little does my lady dream/Charlie Bat is my name."

"What the heck?"

"From 'Rumpelstiltskin.'"

"You are crazy, you know that? No wonder I'm so crazy. How'd you get them to me?"

He smiled and pulled me close to him. He smelled bitter, like cigarettes and coffee, but the smell was warm and comforted me because it brought back all of his embraces, since the day I was born. "I had a little help? There are guardian angels everywhere. Even a few living in the Starlight."

"Guardian angels?" I said. "Do you mean Winter?"

"Winter, spring, summer, fall. It's just a figure of speech, love." He winked at me. "But you do have some nice neighbors."

"And a few creepy ones," I said. "Or at least we did."

"There's always some creepy ones."

"But why did you write the notes at all?"

"I thought it might be good for you in some way, help you grow a little since I couldn't be there to take you places. I thought it might be fun."

"Freaky mimes and evil Tomato Heads aren't fun. And you could have just given me the plane ticket instead of making me wait all those months."

He kissed my cheek. "I guess I needed to get ready for you, too."

The air never cooled for the entire time I was there. It hung over us so thickly, stinking of garbage. The heat seemed to effect the sound levels, making every construction site and honking horn and subway train louder as noise bounced off the wall of humidity.

Still, I loved being with Charlie. We rested in his tiny brownstone apartment during the day and at night when the heat seemed romantic instead of wicked, we walked everywhere. We had gnocchi and ravioli, Indian curries and samosas, pork buns and chow mein. We visited the museum that felt strange and magical at night, like a fairy palace, chamber music drifting through the great hall from some unseen source. We visited the elegant shops and the small boutiques and my dad showed me where the beat poets used to gather and where the new music scene was coming alive at Max's Kansas City and CBGB. I stayed for two weeks but I missed Monroe and my city and my mom and so even though I was sad to leave Charlie I was ready. I had started counting off the time until my return on the second day when the garbage smells rose up like monsters while we went to buy oranges, milk, and cornflakes at the corner market. My father's apartment felt cramped and hot and I longed for Los Angeles with its smog and flowers. I just wished he'd come there, too.

I didn't ask my dad about Annabelle and Hypatia—not once. I didn't want to hear what he had to say. Maybe it wasn't true anyway, I thought. Annabelle was crazy and could have made up anything. Maybe she was some kind of demon, some manifestation of the angry, lost part of myself. Now my business was forgetting. And imagining.

I imagined that when I got back to school in the fall I would have new friends, really cool friends like Skye and Karma Grier, but ones who would never leave me. I closed my eyes and saw a tall, dark, handsome boy who looked scary but was really quite shy and gentle and a cute blonde surfer boy with a funny, snorty laugh and the easiest shoulders. I imagined a boy with dreadlocks and a girl with hair like flowers. And I thought of a boy in a fedora hat and a trench coat, like a funny detective, like a secret agent man, with green eyes that were full of mystery and familiarity at the same time. I saw us all sitting around eating lunch together and laughing. Maybe we would be friends forever. Maybe we would all live together someday, in a sunny cottage like the one I lived in when I was born.

When I got back to L.A. and started school again, none of my imaginary friends showed up. I felt even more sharply that Lily and Bobby and Winter were gone and that they wouldn't be coming back.

But I was a kid and I had already lost pretty much

everything so I decided to just go on as if I hadn't, as if everything was okay. That's what kids can do.

One good thing: Annabelle was gone. Also I still had my mom and Monroe and I had my dad every so often. He visited and took me out to dinner and told me he loved me and I got to visit him in the summer. That was better than some kids had. I had a new sewing machine from Charlie for Christmas and roller skates to take me where I wanted to go. I had this city and I decided that I had better fall in love with her again because she wasn't going anywhere and neither was I.

The black pavement, dark to hide the dirt, sparkled with diamond chips in the burning sun. Poisonous but gorgeous flowers bloomed in white, coral, magenta, and red. The sunsets in L.A. were pink with smog. At night the lethal freeways became the Milky Way.

No matter how bad things get, you can always see the beauty in them. The worse things get, the more you have to make yourself see the magic in order to survive.

ACKNOWLEDGMENTS

Thanks to Charlotte Zolotow and Joanna Cotler for publishing *Weetzie Bat*, my editor Tara Weikum, and everyone at Harper.

SEE HOW WEETZIE'S STORY UNFOLDS
IN *WEETZIE BAT*

*O*nce upon a time in a land called Shangri-L.A., a bleach-blonde punk pixie named Weetzie Bat lived a life of surf and slam until three wishes changed her life forever. . . .

WEETZIE AND DIRK

The reason Weetzie Bat hated high school was because no one understood. They didn't even realize where they were living. They didn't care that Marilyn's prints were practically in their backyard at Graumann's; that you could buy tomahawks and plastic palm tree wallets at Farmer's Market, and the wildest, cheapest cheese and bean and hot dog and pastrami burritos at Oki Dogs; that the waitresses wore skates at the Jetson-style Tiny Naylor's; that there was a fountain that turned tropical soda-pop colors, and a canyon where Jim Morrison and Houdini used to live, and all-night potato knishes at Canter's, and not too far away was Venice, with columns, and canals, even, like the real Venice but maybe cooler because of the surfers. There was no one who cared. Until Dirk.

Dirk was the best-looking guy at school. He wore his hair in a shoe-polish-black Mohawk and he drove a red '55 Pontiac. All the girls were infatuated with Dirk; he wouldn't pay any attention to them. But on the first day of the semester, Dirk saw Weetzie in his art class. She was a skinny girl with a bleach-blonde flat-top. Under the pink Harlequin sunglasses, strawberry lipstick, earrings dangling charms, and sugar-frosted eye shadow she was really almost beautiful. Sometimes she wore Levi's with white-suede fringe sewn down the legs and a feathered Indian headdress, sometimes old fifties' taffeta dresses covered with poetry written in glitter, or dresses made of kids' sheets printed with pink piglets or Disney characters.

"That's a great outfit," Dirk said. Weetzie was wearing her feathered headdress and her moccasins and a pink fringed mini dress.

"Thanks. I made it," she said, snapping her strawberry bubble gum. "I'm into Indians," she said. "They were here first and we treated them like shit."

"Yeah," Dirk said, touching his Mohawk. He smiled. "You want to go to a movie tonight? There's a Jayne Mansfield film festival. *The Girl Can't Help It.*"

"Oh, I love that movie!" Weetzie said in her scratch-iest voice.

Weetzie and Dirk saw *The Girl Can't Help It*, and Weetzie practiced walking like Jayne Mansfield and making siren noises all the way to the car.

"This really is the most slinkster-cool car I have ever seen!" she said.

"His name's Jerry," Dirk said, beaming. "Because he reminds me of Jerry Lewis. I think Jerry likes you. Let's go out in him again."

Weetzie and Dirk went to shows at the Starwood, the Whiskey, the Vex, and Cathay de Grande. They drank beers or bright-colored canned Club drinks in Jerry and told each other how cool they were. Then they went into the clubs dressed to kill in sunglasses and leather, jewels and skeletons, rosaries and fur and silver. They held on like waltzers and plunged in slam-ming around the pit below the stage. Weetzie spat on any skinhead who was too rough, but she always got away with it by batting her eyelashes and blowing a bubble with her gum. Sometimes Dirk dove offstage into the crowd. Weetzie hated that, but of course everyone always caught him because, with his black leather and Mohawk and armloads of chain and his dark-smudged eyes, Dirk was the coolest. After the shows, sweaty and shaky, they went to Oki Dogs for a burrito.

In the daytime, they went to matinees on Hollywood Boulevard, had strawberry sundaes with marshmallow topping at Schwab's, or went to the beach. Dirk taught Weetzie to surf. It was her lifelong dream to surf—along with playing the drums in front of a stadium of adoring fans while wearing gorgeous pajamas. Dirk and Weetzie got tan and ate cheese-and-avocado sandwiches on whole-wheat bread and slept on the beach. Sometimes they skated on the boardwalk. Slinkster Dog went with them wherever they went.

When they were tired or needed comforting, Dirk and Weetzie and Slinkster Dog went to Dirk's Grandma Fifi's cottage, where Dirk had lived since his parents died. Grandma Fifi was a sweet, powdery old lady who baked tiny, white, sugar-coated pastries for them, played them tunes on a music box with a little dancing monkey on top, had two canaries she sang to, and had hair Weetzie envied—perfect white hair that sometimes had lovely blue or pink tints. Grandma Fifi had Dirk and Weetzie bring her groceries, show her their new clothes, and answer the same questions over and over again. They felt very safe and close in Fifi's cottage.

"You're my best friend in the whole world," Dirk said to Weetzie one night. They were sitting in Jerry drinking Club coladas with Slinkster Dog curled up between them.

"You're my best friend in the whole world," Weetzie said to Dirk.

Slinkster Dog's stomach gurgled with pleasure. He was very happy, because Weetzie was so happy now and her new friend Dirk let him ride in Jerry as long as he didn't pee, and they gave him pizza pie for dinner instead of that weird meat that Weetzie's mom, Brandy-Lynn, tried to dish out when he was left at home.

One night, Weetzie and Dirk and Slinkster Dog were driving down Sunset in Jerry on their way to the Odyssey. Weetzie was leaning out the window holding Rubber Chicken by his long, red toe. The breeze was filling Rubber Chicken so that he blew up like a fat, pocked balloon.

At the stoplight, a long, black limo pulled up next to Jerry. The driver leaned out and looked at Rubber Chicken.

"That is one bald-looking chicken!"

The driver threw something into the car and it landed on Weetzie's lap. She screamed.

"What is it?" Dirk exclaimed.

A hairy, black thing was perched on Weetzie's knees.

"It's a hairpiece for that bald eagle you've got there. Belonged to Burt Reynolds," the driver said, and he drove off.

Weetzie put the toupee on Rubber Chicken. Really, it looked quite nice. It made Rubber Chicken look just like the lead singer of a heavy-metal band. Dirk and Weetzie wondered how they could have let him go bald for so long.

"Weetzie, I have something to tell you," Dirk said.

"What?"

"I have to wait till we get to the Odyssey."

At the Odyssey, Weetzie and Dirk bought a pack of cigarettes and two Cokes. Dirk poured rum from the little bottle he kept in his jacket pocket into the Cokes. They sat next to the d.j. booth watching the Lanka girls in spandy-wear dancing around.

"What were you going to tell me?" Weetzie asked.

"I'm gay," Dirk said.

"Who, what, when, where, how—well, not how," Weetzie said. "It doesn't matter one bit, honey-honey," she said, giving him a hug.

Dirk took a swig of his drink. "But you know I'll always love you the best and think you are a beautiful, sexy girl," he said.

"Now we can Duck hunt together," Weetzie said, taking his hand.